THE CHALK CIRCLE MAN

Fred Vargas

The Chalk
Circle Man

TRANSLATED
FROM THE FRENCH
BY

Siân Reynolds

Harvill *Secker*

LONDON

Published by Harvill Secker 2009

2 4 6 8 10 9 7 5 3

First published with the title L'Homme aux cercles bleus in 1996
by Éditions Viviane Hamy, Paris

First published in Great Britain in 2009 by
HARVILL SECKER
Random House
20 Vauxhall Bridge Road
London SW1V 2SA

www.rbooks.co.uk

Addresses for companies within The Random House Group Limited can be found at:
www.randomhouse.co.uk/offices.htm

The Random House Group Limited Reg. No. 954009

A CIP catalogue record for this book is available from the British Library

ISBN 9781843432722

This book is supported by the French Ministry of Foreign Affairs as part of the Burgess
programme run by the Cultural Department of the French Embassy in London.
www.frenchbooknews.com

Liberté · Égalité · Fraternité
RÉPUBLIQUE FRANÇAISE

Ouvrage publié avec le soutien du Centre national du livre – ministère français chargé de la culture

This book is published with support from the French Ministry of Culture –
Centre National du Livre

The Random House Group Limited supports The Forest Stewardship Council (FSC), the leading
international forest certification organisation. All our titles that are printed on Greenpeace
approved FSC certified paper carry the FSC logo. Our paper procurement policy can be found at
www.rbooks.co.uk/environment

Mixed Sources
Product group from well-managed
forests and other controlled sources
www.fsc.org Cert no. TT-COC-2139
© 1996 Forest Stewardship Council
FSC

Typeset in Minion by Palimpsest Book Production Limited
Grangemouth, Stirlingshire
Printed and bound in Great Britain by
CPI Mackays, Chatham ME5 8TD

THE CHALK CIRCLE MAN

I

MATHILDE TOOK OUT HER DIARY AND WROTE: 'THE MAN SITTING next to me has got one hell of a nerve.'

She sipped her beer and glanced once more at the neighbour on her left, a strikingly tall man who had been drumming his fingers on the café table for the past ten minutes.

She made another note in the diary: 'He sat down too close to me, as if we knew each other, but I've never seen him before. No, I'm sure I've never seen him before. Not much else to say about him, except that he's wearing dark glasses. I'm sitting on the terrace outside the Café Saint-Jacques, and I've ordered a glass of draught lager. I'm drinking it now. I'm concentrating as hard as I can on the beer. Can't think of anything better to do.'

Mathilde's neighbour went on drumming his fingers.

'Something the matter?' she asked.

Mathilde had a deep and very husky voice. The man guessed that here was a woman who smoked as much as she could get away with.

'No, nothing. Why?' he replied.

'Just that it's getting on my nerves, that noise you're

making on the tabletop. Everything's setting my teeth on edge today.'

Mathilde finished her beer. Tasteless. Typical for a Sunday. Mathilde considered that she suffered more than most from the fairly widespread malaise she called seventh-day blues.

'You're about fifty, I'd guess?' offered the man, without moving away from her.

'Might be,' said Mathilde.

She felt annoyed. What business was that of his? Just then, she had noticed that the stream of water from the fountain opposite the café was blowing in the wind and sprinkling drops on the arm of the stone cherub beneath: one of those little moments of eternity. And now here was some character spoiling the only moment of eternity of this particular seventh day.

Besides, people usually thought she looked ten years younger. As she told him.

'Does it matter?' asked the man. 'I can't guess ages the way other people do. But I imagine you're rather beautiful, if I'm not mistaken.'

'Is there something wrong with my face?' asked Mathilde. 'You don't seem very sure about it.'

'It's not that. I certainly do imagine you're beautiful,' the man replied, 'but I won't swear to it.'

'Please yourself,' said Mathilde. 'At any rate, *you*'re very good-looking, and I'll swear to that, if it helps. Well, it always does help, doesn't it? And now I'm going to leave you. I'm too edgy today to sit around talking to people like you.'

'I'm not feeling so calm, either. I was going to see a flat to rent, but it was already taken. What about you?'

'I let somebody I wanted to catch up with get away.'

'A friend?'

'No, a woman I was following in the metro. I'd taken lots of notes, and then, suddenly, I lost her. See what I mean?'

'No, I don't see at all.'

'You're not trying, you mean.'

'Well, obviously I'm not trying.'

'You are. You're *very* trying.'

'Yes, I am trying. And on top of that, I'm blind.'

'Oh, Christ!' said Mathilde. 'I'm so sorry.'

The man turned towards her with a rather unkind smile.

'Why are you sorry?' he said. 'It's not your fault, is it?'

Mathilde told herself that she should just stop talking. But she also knew that she wouldn't be able to manage that.

'Whose fault is it, then?' she asked.

The Beautiful Blind Man, as Mathilde had already named him in her head, reverted to his position, three-quarters turned away.

'It was a lioness's fault. I was dissecting it, because I was working on the locomotive system of the larger cats. Why the heck should we care about their locomotive system? Sometimes I would tell myself this is really cutting-edge stuff, other times I thought, oh for God's sake, lions walk, they crouch, they pounce, and that's it. Then one day I made a false move with a scalpel . . .'

'And it squirted in your eyes.'

'Yes. How did you know?'

'There was this man once, he built the colonnade of the Louvre, and he was killed like that. A decomposed camel, laid out on a dissecting table. Still, that was a long time ago, and it was a camel. Quite a big difference, really.'

3

'Well, rotten flesh is still rotten flesh. The ghastly muck went in my eyes. Everything went black. Couldn't see a thing. Kaput.'

'All because of a wretched lioness. I came across a creature like that once. How long ago was this?'

'Eleven years now. She must be laughing her head off, the lioness, wherever she is. Well, I can laugh, sometimes, these days. Not at the time though. A month later I went back and trashed the lab – I threw bits of rotten tissue everywhere, I wanted it to go in everyone's eyes. I smashed up the work of the team studying feline locomotion. But of course it gave me no satisfaction at all. In fact, it was a big let-down.'

'What colour were your eyes?'

'Black, like swifts, the sickles of the sky.'

'And now what are they like?'

'Nobody dares tell me. Black, red and white, I should think. People seem to choke when they see them. I suppose it's a nasty sight. I just keep my glasses on all the time now.'

'I'd like to see them,' said Mathilde, 'if you really want to know what they look like. Nasty sights don't bother me.'

'People say that, then they regret it.'

'When I was diving one day, I got bitten on the leg by a shark.'

'OK, I suppose that's not a pretty sight either.'

'What do you miss the most from not being able to see?'

'Your questions are getting on my nerves. We're not going to spend all day talking about lions and sharks and suchlike beasts, are we?'

'No, I suppose not.'

'Well, if you must know, I miss girls. Not very original, is it?'

'The girls cleared off, did they, after the lioness?'

'Looks like that. You didn't say why you were following the woman.'

'No reason. I follow lots of people, actually. Can't help it, it's an addiction.'

'After the shark bite, did your lover clear off?'

'He left, and others came along.'

'You're an unusual woman.'

'Why do you say that?' asked Mathilde.

'Because of your voice.'

'What do you hear in people's voices?'

'Oh, come on, I'm not going to tell you that! What would I have left, for pity's sake? You've got to let a blind man have some advantages, madame,' said the man, with a smile.

He stood up to leave. He hadn't even finished his drink.

'Wait. What's your name?' Mathilde asked.

The man hesitated.

'Charles Reyer,' he said.

'Thank you. My name's Mathilde.'

The Beautiful Blind Man said that was a rather classy name, that there was a queen called Mathilde who had reigned in England in the twelfth century. Then he walked off, guiding himself with a finger along the wall. Mathilde couldn't care less about the twelfth century, and she finished the blind man's drink, with a frown.

For a long time afterwards, for weeks during her excursions along the pavements of Paris, Mathilde looked out for the blind man, out of the corner of her eye. But she didn't find him. She guessed his age as about thirty-five.

II

HE HAD JUST BEEN APPOINTED TO PARIS, *COMMISSAIRE* OF THE police headquarters in the 5th *arrondissement*. And on day twelve, he was on his way to his new office, on foot.

Paris had been a stroke of luck. The only city in France for which he could feel affection. For a long time, he had thought that where he lived was a matter of indifference, like the food he ate, the furniture around him, or the clothes he wore – all either donated or inherited, or picked up here and there.

But in the end, deciding where to live wasn't so simple. As a child, Jean-Baptiste Adamsberg had run around barefoot in the stony foothills of the Pyrenees. He had lived and slept there, and later, after becoming a policeman, he had been obliged to work on murders committed there, murders in the stone-built villages, murders on the rocky paths. He knew by heart the sound of pebbles underfoot and the mountain's way of gripping you and clutching you to its heart like a muscular old man. In the police station where he had started working at twenty-five, they had called him 'the wild child'. Perhaps this was a reference to his being primitive, or solitary – he wasn't sure. He found it neither original nor flattering.

He had asked the reason once, from one of the younger women inspectors – his direct superior, whom he would have liked to kiss, but since she was ten years older than him he hadn't dared. She was embarrassed and had said: 'Work it out, look at yourself in the mirror, you'll get there on your own.' That evening he had looked – without any pleasure, since he liked tall pale people – at his small, solid, dark-complexioned figure, and the next day he said: 'I stood in front of the mirror and looked, but I still didn't understand what you meant.'

'Oh, Adamsberg,' the inspector had said, rather wearily and with some exasperation, 'why do you say things like that? Why do you ask questions? We're working on a case about stolen watches, that's all there is to know. I'm not going to start talking about your body.' She had added: 'I'm not paid to talk about your body'.

'OK,' Jean-Baptiste had said. 'No need to get worked up about it.'

An hour later, he heard the typewriter stop and the inspector had called him in. She was looking cross. 'Let's just have it out once and for all,' she said. 'You have the body of a child of nature, that's what it is.' He had replied, 'Do you mean it's primitive? Ugly?' She looked even more exasperated. 'Don't push me to tell you that you're good-looking, Adamsberg,' she had said. 'But you have a certain grace about you that's unique – you'll just have to get used to that in your life.' And there had been both weariness and tenderness in her voice, of that he had been sure. So that, even now, he recalled the conversation with a pleasurable shiver, especially since it had never reached that degree of intimacy again. He had waited for it to go further, with his heart racing. Perhaps she was going to kiss him. Perhaps. But she kept her distance and never spoke of it again. Except once, in despair: 'You're not cut out for the police, Jean-Baptiste. There's no room for wild creatures like you in the police.'

Well, she had been wrong. Over the next five years, he had solved, one after another, four murders in a way that his colleagues had found uncanny, in other words unfair and provocative. 'Don't get above yourself, Adamsberg,' they'd said. 'You sit around daydreaming, staring at the wall, or doodling on a bit of paper as if you had all the time and knowledge in the world, and then one day you swan in, cool as cucumber, and say "Arrest the priest. He strangled the child to stop him talking."'

So the wild child who had solved four murders found himself promoted to inspector, then to *commissaire*, but he was still inclined to doodle for hours, resting pieces of paper on his knee, scoring the fabric of his nondescript trousers. Two weeks ago, he had been offered a posting to Paris. He had left behind him office walls covered with graffiti which he had scribbled there over the last twenty years, without ever getting tired of life.

But how weary of other people he sometimes felt! It was as if, all too often, he knew in advance exactly what he was going to hear. And every time that he thought: 'This person is going to say such-and-such now', he hated himself, especially when the person in question did say exactly that. Then he suffered, begging some god to give him a surprise one day, instead of foreknowledge.

Sitting in a café across the street from his new office, Jean-Baptiste Adamsberg stirred his coffee. Did he know now why they called him the wild child? Yes, it had become a little clearer, but people weren't very careful how they used words. He was particularly bad at it himself. What was certain was that Paris was the only place that could provide him with the mineral surroundings that he realised were important to him.

Paris, city of stone.

There were trees, of course, inevitably, but you could ignore them, you just had to avoid looking at them. And there were parks, but you simply kept out of them, and that was fine too. By way of vegetation, Adamsberg preferred straggling shrubs and root crops. What also seemed certain was that he hadn't changed much over the years, since the expressions on the faces of his new colleagues reminded him of his fellow officers in the Pyrenees twenty years ago: the same discreet bafflement, the same whispers behind his back, nods of complicity, pulled faces, fingers splayed in gestures of surrender. So many silent communications that seemed to say: 'Who *is* this character?'

He had gently smiled and shaken hands, gently explained and listened. Adamsberg did everything gently. But he was eleven days in now, and his colleagues were still not approaching him without that look: one that suggested they were trying to work out what kind of species they were dealing with, what it should be given to eat, how it should be spoken to, how one might amuse or interest it. For eleven days, the 5th *arrondissement* station had been plunged into whispers, as if some fragile mystery had suspended ordinary police routines.

The difference between this situation and Adamsberg's early days in the Pyrenees was that nowadays his reputation made things a bit easier. However, that still didn't alter the fact that he was an outsider. The day before, he had overheard the oldest Parisian in the team saying in a low voice: 'Ah well, he's from the Pyrenees – pretty much the edge of the known world.'

He ought to have been at the office half an hour ago, but Adamsberg was still sitting across the road, stirring his coffee.

It wasn't that he permitted himself to turn up at work late just because, nowadays, at the age of forty-five, he had won the respect of those around him. He had already been turning up late at twenty. Even for his own birth, he had been sixteen days late. Adamsberg didn't wear a watch, but he was unable to say why, and he had nothing against watches. Or umbrellas. Or anything else, really. It wasn't so much that he did as he pleased, more that he was unable to force himself to do something if he was in a contrary mood at that moment. He had never been able to do that, even in the days when he had wanted to attract the beautiful police inspector. Even for her. People had said resignedly that Adamsberg was a lost cause, and he sometimes thought the same himself. Not always, though.

And today his mood pushed him to sit stirring his coffee, slowly. A textile merchant had been killed three days earlier, in his own warehouse. His accounts had looked so irregular that three inspectors were going through the customer files, convinced that the murderer's name would be found there.

Ever since he had seen the dead man's family, Adamsberg had not felt too concerned about this case. His inspectors were searching for a client who'd been cheated, and they even had one serious lead, but he had been keeping an eye on the murdered man's stepson, Patrice Vernoux, a fine-featured, romantic-looking young man of twenty-three. That was all Adamsberg had done: keep an eye on him. He had already called him in three times to the station on different pretexts, getting him to talk about this and that: what did he think of his stepfather's bald patch – did it disgust him? Did he like the textile business? What did he think when the electricity workers went on strike, why did he think so many people were interested in their family tree?

The last time, the day before, it had gone as follows:

'Do you think you're good-looking?' Adamsberg had asked.

'It's hard to say no.'

'You're right.'

'Can you tell me why I'm here?'

'Yes. Because of your stepfather, of course. You did tell me you didn't like to think of him sleeping with your mother.'

The young man shrugged.

'Nothing I could do about it, was there? Except kill him, and I didn't do that. But yeah, it did make me feel a bit sick. My stepfather was gross, he was hairy, he even had hair coming out of his ears, like a, well, a wild boar. Tell you the truth, monsieur, I couldn't stomach that. Would you?'

'Oh, I don't know. One day I walked in on my own mother in bed with one of my ex-schoolfriends. And yet, poor woman, she was faithful on the whole. I closed the door, and I remember that the only thing I thought was that the boy had an olive-green mole on his back, but perhaps my mother hadn't seen it.'

'Don't see what that has to do with me,' said the boy, sulkily. 'If you can take that kind of thing better than me, that's your business.'

'Never mind – it doesn't matter. Is your mother upset, do you think?'

'Naturally she is.'

'OK. Fine. But don't go and see too much of her for now.'
And he had let the boy go.

Adamsberg walked into the station. Of his inspectors at present, his favourite was Adrien Danglard, a man who dressed impeccably in order to compensate for his unprepossessing looks and pear-shaped figure. Danglard liked a drink and didn't seem too reliable after about four in the afternoon, or even earlier sometimes. But he was real, very real, and Adamsberg hadn't yet found any other way of defining him to himself. Danglard had prepared a summary of the inquiry into the textile firm's customer files.

'Danglard, I'd like to see the stepson today – the boy, Patrice Vernoux.'

'Again, *monsieur le commissaire*? Why do you keep going after the poor lad?'

'Why do you call him a poor lad?'

'Because he's shy, he keeps combing his hair, he tries to help, he's doing his best to say what you want, and when he's waiting in that corridor and doesn't know what you're going to ask him next, he looks so lost that I feel sorry for him. That's why I call him a poor lad.'

'You didn't notice anything else, Danglard?'

Danglard shook his head.

'Have I told you the story about the dog that drooled?' Adamsberg asked.

'No, I must say you haven't.'

'When you've heard it, you'll think I'm a mean bastard. You'll have to sit down: I can't talk fast, I have trouble finding the right words and I sometimes lose the thread. I'm not very articulate, Danglard. So anyway, I went out of our village very early one morning to spend the day in the mountains – this was when I was about eleven. I don't like dogs and I didn't like them when I was little, either. And this one, a big dog with drooling chops, was just standing in the middle of the path, looking at me. It drooled all over my feet and hands, it was just a friendly, soppy old dog. I said to it: "Look, dog, I'm going for a long walk, what I'm trying to do is get lost and then find my way back. You can come with me if you want, but stop drooling all over me, it's disgusting." Well, the dog seemed to understand and started following me.'

Adamsberg stopped, lit a cigarette, and took a scrap of paper out of his pocket. He crossed his legs and rested the paper on his thigh to scribble a drawing, then went on, after a glance at his colleague.

'Can't help it if I'm boring you, Danglard, but I do want to tell you the story about the dog. So this dog and I set off, chatting about whatever interested us – the stars in the sky or juicy bones – and we stopped at an old shepherd's hut. And there we came face to face with half a dozen kids from another village, I knew who they were, we'd had fights in the past. They said, "This your dog?" I said: "Just for today." Then the smallest of them got hold of the dog by its long fur, because this dog was as cowardly and soft as a hearthrug, and he pulled it to the edge of an overhang. "Don't like your fucking dog," he said. "Stupid fucking dog." The big dog was whining, but it wasn't reacting, it's true that it was stupid. And this tiny kid gave it a big kick up the backside, and the dog went over the edge. I put my bag down slowly. I do everything slowly. I'm a slow man, Danglard.'

Yes, Danglard felt like saying, I had noticed. A vague man, a slow man. But he couldn't say that, since Adamsberg was his new boss. And anyway, he respected him. Danglard, like everyone else, had heard rumours of Adamsberg's famous cases and, like everyone else, he admired the way he had solved them, something which today seemed to him incompatible with the man himself, as he had turned out on his arrival in Paris. Now that he had seen him in the flesh, he was surprised, and not only by his slow movements and way of talking. He was also disappointed by the unimpressive appearance of Adamsberg's small, thin, yet compact body, and by the generally casual manner of this person who had not even turned up at the appointed time to meet the staff and who, when he did, had evidently hastily knotted on a necktie over a shapeless shirt stuffed negligently into the waistband of his trousers.

And then Adamsberg's charm had started to work, rising like the water level. It had started with his voice. Danglard liked to listen to him: it calmed him – indeed, almost put him to sleep. 'It's like a caress,' Florence had said, but then Florence was a woman, and anyway she was responsible for her choice of words. Castreau had snorted: 'Don't go telling us next that he's good-looking.' Florence had looked puzzled. 'Wait a bit, I need to think about that,' she had said. As she always did. She was a scrupulous person who took time to think before she spoke. Not feeling sure, she had murmured, 'No, but it has to do with a kind of grace. I'll think some more about it.' When the other colleagues had laughed at her serious expression, Danglard had said, 'Yes, Florence is right, it's obvious.' Margellon, a young officer, had seized the opportunity to call Danglard a poof. Margellon had never made an intelligent remark in his life. And Danglard needed intelligence as much as he needed drink. He had shrugged his shoulders, thinking briefly that it was a pity Margellon wasn't right, because he had always had bad luck with women, and perhaps men would have been less fussy. He had heard it said that men were bastards, because once they had slept with a woman they passed judgement on her, but women were worse, because they refused to sleep with you unless everything was exactly right. So not only were you weighed up and judged, but you never got to sleep with anyone.

Sad, really.

Yes, women were complicated. And in Danglard's life there had been plenty of women who had found him wanting. To his considerable distress at times. But at any rate, he knew that serious-minded Florence was right about Adamsberg, and Danglard had so far allowed himself to succumb to the charm of this little man a foot shorter than himself. He was beginning to understand how the vague desire to unburden yourself to him might explain why so many murderers had told him about their crimes: absent-mindedly, almost. Just like that. In order to chat to Adamsberg.

Danglard, who had a reputation for being handy with a pencil, did caricatures of his colleagues. So he knew something about faces. He had got Castreau off to a T, for instance. But he knew in advance that he would never be able to pin Adamsberg down, because it was as if sixty faces had been mingled to make one. The nose was too big, the mouth was crooked, mobile, and no doubt sensual, the eyes were vague and elusive, the jawbone was too prominent, so it looked as if it would be easy to caricature this mixed-up face, thrown together with disregard for classical harmony. It was as if God had run out of raw materials when he had made Jean-Baptiste Adamsberg: he had had to look in the back of the drawer and put together features that should never have been combined if he'd had more choice. But after that, it looked as if God had been aware of the problem and had taken special care, a great deal of care, in fact, and in the end had created an inexplicable masterpiece out of this face. And Danglard, who could not remember ever having seen a face like it, considered that trying to make a rapid sketch of it would be a travesty, that swift pencil strokes would not bring out its originality: on the contrary, a sketch would destroy all its grace.

So at that moment, Danglard was wondering what sort of things God kept in the back of the drawer.

'Are you listening, or have you gone to sleep?' Adamsberg asked. 'Because I've noticed that I sometimes send people to sleep, really, they do go to sleep. Perhaps I don't speak loudly enough, or fast enough, I don't know. Remember where we'd got to? The dog had gone over the edge. I took my tin water bottle off my belt and banged the little kid hard on the head.

'And then I set off to find the stupid dog. It took me three hours to reach it. And by then it was dead, anyway. The point of this story, Danglard, is the evidence of cruelty in that little kid. I'd known for a long time before this happened that there was something wrong with him, and that was what it was: cruelty. But I can assure you his face was quite normal, he didn't have wicked features at all. On the contrary, he was a nice-looking boy, but he oozed cruelty. Just don't ask me any more, I can't tell you any more. But eight years later, he pushed a grandfather clock over on top of an old woman and killed her. And most premeditated murders require the murderer not only to feel exasperation or humiliation, or to have some neurosis, or whatever, but also cruelty, pleasure in inflicting suffering, pleasure in the victim's agony and pleas for mercy, pleasure in tearing the victim apart. It's true, it doesn't always appear obvious in a person, but you feel at least that there's something wrong, that something else is gathering underneath, a kind of growth. And sometimes that turns out to be cruelty – do you see what I'm saying? A kind of growth.'

'That's against my principles,' said Danglard, a bit stiffly. 'I don't claim my principles are the only ones, but I don't believe there are people marked out for this or that, like cows with tags on their ears, or that you can pick out murderers by intuition. I know, I'm saying something boring and unexciting, but what we do is we proceed by following clues, and we arrest when we've got proof. Gut feelings about "growths" scare me stiff. That way you start off following hunches, and end up with arbitrary sentences and miscarriages of justice.'

'You're speechifying, Danglard. I didn't say you could see it in someone's face, I said it was something monstrous that was gathering inside someone. It's a kind of secretion, Danglard, and sometimes I sense it oozing out. I've seen it on the lips of a young girl, just as clearly as I might see a cockroach run across this table. I can't help sensing when something's not right. It might be enjoyment of crime, but it could be other things, less serious things. Some people secrete their boredom or their unhappy love lives, Danglard, and it can be sensed, whether it's the one or the other. But when it's something else, you know, the crime thing, well, I think I know that too.'

Danglard looked up and his posture was less shambling than usual.

'Yes, but you still believe you can see something by looking at people, that you can see cockroaches on their lips, and you think these impressions are revelations because they're yours, you think other people are oozing pus, and it's not true. The truth is boring and banal: it's that all human beings can have hate inside them, like they all have hair on their heads, and anyone can make a false step and kill someone. I'm certain of that. All men are capable of rape and murder, and all women are capable of slashing someone's legs with a razor, like that one in the rue Gay-Lussac the other week. It just depends what sort of life you've had, it depends how much you want to plunge into the swamp and take other people with you. You don't have to be oozing pus from birth to want to suppress the whole world because you're sick of it.'

'I did tell you, Danglard,' said Adamsberg, frowning, as he stopped his drawing, 'that when I'd told you the story of the big dog you'd think I was a mean bastard.'

'Dangerous, let's say,' muttered Danglard. 'You shouldn't think you've got some superior powers.'

'There's nothing superior about being able to see cockroaches. What I'm telling you about is something that I can't help. In fact, it gives me enormous trouble in my life. If only I could be wrong about someone once in a while, about whether he was an upright citizen or not, or sad, or intelligent, or untruthful, or troubled, or indifferent, or dangerous, or timid – all that, do you see, if I could just be wrong one time, for a change? Can you imagine what a drag it is? I sometimes pray that people will surprise me when I start to predict how it will all end. All my life I've always had beginnings, and I've been full of hope. And then, very soon, I start to see what's going to happen, like in some suspense film where you guess who's going to fall in love with whom, or who's going to have an accident. You go on watching all the same, only it's too late – it's just depressing.'

'OK, let's admit you have some special intuition,' said Danglard. 'You're a policeman with flair, that's as far as I'll go. But even then it's not right to use it, it's too risky, it's wicked. No, even after twenty years you can never know everything about another person.'

Adamberg rested his chin on his palm, smoke from his cigarette making his eyes water.

'Well, if it's a gift take it away from me, Danglard. Get rid of it. I'd like nothing better.'

'People aren't insects,' Danglard went on.

'No, they're not. I like people, and I don't give a damn about insects, don't care what they want or what they think. Still, insects want things too, no reason they shouldn't.'

'True,' said Danglard.

'Danglard, have you ever been party to a miscarriage of justice yourself?'

'Have you read my file?' said Danglard, with a sideways glance at Adamsberg who was still smoking and doodling.

'If I say no, you'll accuse me of claiming supernatural powers. But no, I haven't read it. What happened?'

'It was this teenage girl. There'd been a break-in at the jeweller's shop where she worked. I was absolutely convinced it was an inside job, done with her collusion. Everything seemed to point to it. Her prevarications, her mannerisms, all that set off my policeman's intuition, OK? She got three years, and she committed suicide in her cell two months later, in a particularly ghastly way. But in fact she hadn't been involved in the robbery, as we discovered not long afterwards. So now do you see why I won't have anything to do with your blasted hunches and cockroaches on women's lips? Finito. After that, I decided guesswork and intuition were no match for doubt and ordinary police routine.'

Danglard stood up.

'Wait,' said Adamsberg. 'The stepson, Vernoux – don't forget to bring him in.'

Adamsberg fell silent. He was embarrassed. His decision was awkward coming after this kind of discussion. He went on in a lower voice.

'Pull him in for questioning for twenty-four hours.'

'You're not serious, *commissaire*,' said Danglard.

Adamsberg bit his lower lip.

'His girlfriend's protecting him. I'm convinced they weren't actually together in the restaurant on the evening of the murder, even if their two versions tally. Question them again, separately. How long between the starter and the main course? Did a guitarist come and play? Where was the wine, on the left or the right of the table? What kind of wine was it? What did the glasses look like, or the tablecloth? And so on – every little detail you can think of. They'll end up saying different things, you'll see. And then check out the boy's shoes. You can ask the cleaning woman who comes in and looks after him – his mother pays her. There'll be a pair missing, the ones he wore on the night of the murder, because round the warehouse the ground's very muddy, what with the building site alongside it, and the mud there is clay – it sticks like glue. He's not stupid, our young man, he's probably chucked the shoes away. Have someone check the drains near where he lives. He could have walked back the last stretch in his socks, between the drain and his front door.'

'If I understand what you're saying,' Danglard said, 'the poor lad, as I call him, is oozing something.'

'I'm afraid so,' said Adamsberg quietly.

'And what is he supposed to be oozing?'

'Cruelty.'

'And to you that's obvious?'

'Yes, Danglard.'

But the last two words were almost inaudible.

Once the inspector had left, Adamsberg pulled across his desk the pile of newspapers that had been prepared for him. He found what he was after in three of them. The phenomenon hadn't reached the headlines yet, but it was surely only a matter of time. Clumsily, he tore out one short article and put it on the desk in front of him. He always needed to concentrate hard in order to read, and if he had to do it out loud it was even worse. Adamsberg had never shone at school, since he couldn't really understand why they were making him turn up there at all, but he had tried to give the impression of being conscientious so as not to upset his parents, and in particular so that they would never find out that he didn't really care for book learning.

Is this a practical joke, or the work of some half-baked philosopher? Whatever it is, the blue chalk circles are still sprouting like night-time weeds on the capital's pavements, and they're starting to attract the attention of Parisian intellectuals. The circles are turning up at an increasing rate. Sixty-three have been spotted since the first ones were found four months ago in the 12th arrondissement. This new distraction, the equivalent of an urban parlour game, has provided plenty of material for the chattering classes, of whom there is no shortage. So the circles are the talk of every café in town . . .

Adamsberg stopped reading and jumped to the end to read the byline. 'That pretentious prat,' he muttered. 'What can you expect?'

. . . People will soon be jostling for the honour of finding a circle outside their door, on the way to work in the morning. Whether the circles are the work of a cynical con artist or a genuine madman, if it's fame he's after the creator of the circles has certainly got what he wanted. Galling, isn't it, for people who've spent a lifetime trying to become famous? All you have to do to be Parisian celebrity of the year is go out at night with some blue chalk! If he's ever tracked down, they'll have him on a TV chat show in no time (I can see it now: 'The cultural sensation of the fin-de-millennium'). But he's an elusive character. Nobody's yet caught him in the act of chalking his circles on the tarmac. He doesn't venture out every night, and he seems to strike at random in one district of Paris after another. What's the betting there are some night-owls out there trying to catch him, just for kicks? Well, good hunting!

A more thoughtful article had appeared in a provincial paper:

Paris haunted by harmless maniac
Everyone thinks this is good for a laugh, but perhaps 'weird' is a better description. For the last four months, somebody – a man, probably – has been going out at night and drawing large circles in blue chalk around whatever rubbish is lying on the pavements of Paris. The only 'victims' of this curious obsession are the items that this character

encloses within the circles, never more than one at a time. There are about sixty examples so far, which makes it possible to draw up a very peculiar list: twelve bottle tops, an orange-box, four paper clips, two shoes, a magazine, a leather handbag, four cigarette lighters, a handkerchief, a pigeon's claw, a spectacle lens, five notebooks, a lamb-chop bone, a ballpoint pen, an earring, a dog turd, part of a car's headlight, a battery, a Coca-Cola can, a piece of wire, a ball of wool, a keyring, an orange, a tube of stomach pills, a pool of vomit, a hat, the contents of a car's ashtray, two books (The Metaphysics of *the* Real *and* The Fun-to-Cook Book), *a metal label, a broken egg, an 'I love Elvis' badge, a pair of tweezers, a doll's head, a twig, a vest, a roll of film, a vanilla yoghurt, a candle, and a swimming cap. This may seem a tedious kind of list, but it certainly reveals the unexpected treasures lying on the city's pavements if one goes looking for them. Since the well-known psychiatrist René Vercors-Laury has taken an interest in this case from the start, and has been keen to find out what lies behind it, people are now talking about the 'revisited object'. The 'chalk circle man' has become a subject of cocktail-party gossip, putting the poor graffiti artists in the shade – their noses must be really out of joint! Everyone is asking what kind of compulsion drives the chalk circle man. One of the most intriguing aspects of the case is that around the edge of every circle, written in beautiful copperplate, indicating therefore an educated hand, is the following inscription, which has the psychiatrists scratching their heads: 'Victor, woe's in store, what are you out here for?'*

An indistinct photo was attached.

The third article was less detailed and very short, but reported that the previous night another circle had been found in the rue Caulaincourt in northern Paris, this time around a dead mouse, with the same legend: '*Victor, woe's in store, what are you out here for?*'

Adamsberg pulled a face. It was just as he had feared.

He slipped the articles under his desk lamp and decided he was hungry, although he had no idea of the time. He went out, took a long walk along the still-unfamiliar streets, absent-mindedly ordered a sandwich and drink, bought a packet of cigarettes, and made his way slowly back to the station. In his trouser pocket he could feel at every step the crumpled letter from Christiane which had arrived that morning. She wrote on thick expensive notepaper, which was awkward to stuff into your pocket. Adamsberg disliked the paper.

He would have to give her his new address. She wouldn't find it difficult to come and see him often, since she worked in Orleans. But her letter suggested she was looking for a job in Paris. Because of him. He shook his head. He'd think about that later. Since he had met her, six months ago now, it was always the same, he'd think about it later. She wasn't a stupid woman, quite bright in fact, though she did tend to have predictable opinions. A pity, but not too serious, since that was a minor failing and after all nobody's perfect. Ah, but perfection, the impossible, the unpredictable, the softest skin, the perpetual movement between gravity and grace, had come to him only once, eight years earlier, with Camille and her ridiculous pet monkey, a marmoset called Richard III. She used to let the monkey relieve itself in the street, telling any passers-by who objected, 'But you see, Richard III has to go outside to pee.'

The little monkey, who smelled of oranges for some reason, although it never ate them, would sometimes jump onto their arms and make a great show of looking for fleas on their wrists, with a concentrated expression and neat little movements. Camille and Jean-Baptiste joined in the game, scratching at the invisible prey on their forearms. But she had run away, his *petite chérie*. And he, the policeman, had never been able to trace her, despite all the time he had spent searching a whole year, such a long year, and afterwards his youngest sister had said, 'Come on, you don't have any right to do this, leave her in peace!' '*Ma petite chérie*,' Adamsberg had said. 'You want to see her again?' his sister had asked. Only the youngest of his five sisters dared talk to him about his *petite chérie*. And he had smiled and said, 'With all my heart, yes, even if it's just for an hour before I die.'

Adrien Danglard was waiting for him in the office, a plastic cup of white wine in his hand and a combination of mixed emotions on his face.

'The Vernoux boy's boots were missing,' he said. 'Ankle boots with buckles.'

Adamsberg stood silently for a moment. He was trying to respect Danglard's irritation.

'I didn't mean to give you a demonstration this morning,' he said. 'I can't help it if the Vernoux boy's the killer. Did you look for the boots?'

Danglard produced a plastic bag and put it on the table.

'Here they are,' he sighed. 'The lab's started doing tests, but you can see at a glance it's the mud from that building site on the soles, so sticky that the water in the drain didn't wash it off. Pity. Nice shoes.'

'They were in the drain then?'

'Yes, twenty-five metres down from the nearest grating to his house.'

'You're a fast worker, Danglard.'

Silence fell between the two men. Adamsberg was biting his lip. He had picked up a cigarette, taken a pencil stub out his pocket, and flattened a bit of paper over his knee. He was thinking: He's going to give me a lecture now, he's angry and shocked, I should never have told him the story of the dog that drooled, or told him that Patrice Vernoux oozed cruelty like the little kid in the mountains.

But no. Adamsberg looked at his colleague. Danglard's long shambling body, which took the shape of a melted bottle when he sat on a chair, was looking relaxed. He had plunged his large hands deep in the pockets of his elegant suit, and put the wine on the floor. He was staring into space, but even like that Adamsberg could see that he was formidably intelligent. Danglard said:

'Congratulations, *commissaire*.'

Then he got up, as he had done earlier, first bending the top half of his body forward, then lifting his backside off the chair and finally standing up straight.

'I have to tell you,' he added, with his back half-turned to Adamsberg, 'that after four in the afternoon I'm not good for much – best you should know that. So if you want to ask me to do anything, mornings are best. And if you want people for a manhunt, shooting, any of that kind of rubbish, forget it, my hand shakes and my knees give way. Apart from that, my legs and head are usable. I think the head works reasonably well, even if it works very differently from yours. A supercilious colleague told me one day that if I was still in my job as inspector, with the amount of white wine I drink, it's because my bosses have turned a blind eye to it, and because I have two sets of twins at home, which makes four children to bring up as a single parent, on account of my wife having run off with her lover to study the statues on Easter Island. When I was young, twenty-five that is, I wanted to write either a master-piece or nothing: something as good as Chateaubriand's memoirs. You won't be surprised to learn that that didn't work out. OK. Now I'm taking the boots, and I'm going to interview Patrice Vernoux and his girlfriend who are waiting next door.'

'Danglard, I like you,' said Adamsberg, still doodling.

'I think I'd gathered that,' said Danglard, picking up the plastic cup.

'Ask the photographer to make sure he's free tomorrow morning and go along with him. I want a description and some clear pictures of the blue chalk circle that may be drawn somewhere in Paris tonight.'

'A circle? You mean this nutter who draws rings round bottle tops? "*Victor, woe's in store, what are you out here for?*"'

'That's exactly what I mean, Danglard.'

'But it's stupid. What . . .'

Adamsberg shook his head impatiently.

'I know, Danglard, I know. Just do it. Please. And don't tell anyone for the time being.'

After that, Adamsberg finished the sketch that he had been resting on his knee. He could hear raised voices from the next room. Vernoux's girlfriend was cracking. It was obvious that she had had nothing to do with the murder of the elderly businessman. Her only error of judgement, but it had been a serious one, was to have been sufficiently in love with Vernoux, or sufficiently obedient to him, to back up his false alibi. The worst thing for her wouldn't be the court appearance: it was what was happening right now, as she discovered her lover's cruelty.

What on earth had he eaten at midday to give him such a stomach-ache? He couldn't remember. He picked up the telephone to arrange an interview with the psychiatrist, René Vercors-Laury. Tomorrow at eleven, the receptionist suggested. He had given her his name, Jean-Baptiste Adamsberg, and it had opened doors. He was not yet accustomed to this kind of celebrity, although it had been attached to him for some time. But Adamsberg had the feeling that he had no contact with his public image: it was as if there were two of him. Still, since childhood he had always felt there were two people inside him: Jean-Baptiste on the one hand and Adamsberg on the other – both watching what Jean-Baptiste got up to, following his movements with amusement. And now there were three: Jean-Baptiste, Adamsberg, and the public figure with the same name. A holy but shattered trinity. He got up to fetch a coffee from the machine next door, where he would often find Margellon helping himself. But it so happened that just then everyone was there, with a woman who seemed to be causing a loud disturbance. Castreau kept repeating patiently, 'Madame, I think you should leave.'

Adamsberg served himself a coffee and looked round. The woman was speaking in a husky voice; she was both angry and sad. Clearly she was exasperated with the cops. She was dressed in black. Adamsberg decided that she had an Egyptian profile, or perhaps she had other origins that had produced one of those dark aquiline faces you never forget but carry round in your head ever after – not unlike his *petite chérie*, in fact.

Castreau was now saying:

'This isn't a lost-property department, madame. Please be reasonable, and leave now.'

The woman was no longer young. Adamsberg put her somewhere between forty-five and sixty. Her hands were tanned and energetic, with short nails, the hands of a woman who had spent her life somewhere else, using them to search for something.

'So what's the point of the police, then?' the woman was saying, shaking back her dark shoulder-length hair. 'You could make a bit of an effort. It wouldn't kill you, would it, to give me some idea where to look? It might take me ten years to find him, but you could do it in a day!'

This time Castreau lost his cool.

'Look, I don't give a damn about your private life!' he shouted. 'He's not listed as a missing person, is he? So please just go away and leave me in peace – we don't do lonely hearts here. If you go on making a fuss I'll call the boss.'

Adamsberg was leaning against the wall at the back of the room.

'I *am* the boss,' he said, without moving.

Mathilde turned round. She saw a man with hooded eyes looking at her with uncommon gentleness, she registered his shirt, stuffed into one side of his trousers, loose on the other, she saw that his thin face didn't match his hands which seemed to have come from a Rodin statue, and she immediately understood that things would now improve.

Detaching himself from the wall, Adamsberg pushed the door of his office and beckoned her in.

'It's true, of course,' Mathilde said, seating herself, 'this isn't the lost-property office. It's been a bad day. And not much better yesterday, or the day before either . . . A whole section of the week gone to pot. I hope you've had a better section than I have.'

'A section?'

'Well, the way I see it, Monday-Tuesday-Wednesday, that's section number one of the week. What happens in section number one is different from what happens in section number two.'

'And that's Thursday-Friday-Saturday?'

'Of course. If you pay attention, you'll see there are more serious surprises in section one as a rule – note that I'm saying as a *rule* – and more fun and distractions in section two. It's a question of rhythm. It never switches over like the parking in the street, where you have to park one side one week and the other the next. Why do they do that, anyway? To give the street a rest? Let it lie fallow? No idea. Anyway, sections of the week don't change. First section: you're alert, you believe all sorts of stuff, you get things done. It's a miracle of human activity. Second section: you don't find anything you're looking for, you learn nothing new, it's pretty much a waste of time. In the second section there's a lot of this and that, and you drink quite a bit, whereas the first section is more important, obviously. In practice, a section number two can't go far wrong, because it doesn't really matter, so to speak. But when a section number one goes haywire, like this week, it's really horrible. And another thing: the special today in the café was beef and lentils. Beef and lentils is a dish that really depresses me to the point of despair. Right at the end of a section one. Just no luck at all, a wretched plate of lentils.'

'What about Sundays?'

'Oh, Sundays, that's section three. Just that one day takes up a whole section – see how important that is? And section three is the pits. If you get beef and lentils combined with a section three, you might as well go hang yourself.'

'Where were we?' asked Adamsberg, having the sudden, not unpleasant impression that his thoughts could wander even further talking to this woman than when talking to himself.

'We hadn't got anywhere.'

'Right, OK, we've got nowhere.'

'It's coming back to me,' said Mathilde. 'Since my section one was practically a write-off, as I was passing your police station I thought I might as well be hanged for a sheep as a lamb, so I'd give it a go. But you see, it doesn't work – trying to rescue a section one might be tempting, but it gets you nowhere. What about you, anyway?'

'Oh, it's not been a bad week so far,' Adamsberg admitted.

'Now if you'd seen my section one last week, that was terrific.'

'What happened?'

'I can't just tell you like that, I'd have to look it up in my notebook. Still, tomorrow we start a section two, so we can relax a bit.'

'Tomorrow I'm going to see a psychiatrist. Is that a good start for a section two?'

'Good Lord! On your own account?' asked Mathilde in surprise. 'No, of course not, stupid of me. I get the feeling that even if the spirit moved you to piss against all the lamp-posts down one side of the road, you'd say to yourself, "That's the way it is, and God help the lamp-posts," but you wouldn't go and consult a psychiatrist. Sorry, I know I'm talking too much, I'm fed up. I'm getting on my own nerves.'

Mathilde took a cigarette from Adamsberg, saying 'May I?' and pulled off the filter.

'Perhaps you're going to see the psychiatrist about the chalk circle man,' she went on. 'Don't look at me like that – I haven't been snooping. It's just that you've got those newspaper cuttings about him tucked under the base of your lamp, so naturally I wondered.'

'Yes, you're right,' Adamsberg admitted, 'it is about him. Why did you come into the station?'

'I'm looking for this man I don't know.'

'Why are you looking for him, then?'

'Because I don't know him! What a question!'

'Touché,' said Adamsberg.

'I was following this woman in the street, and I lost her. So I ended up in a café, and that's how I met my beautiful blind man. There are an amazing number of people walking round on the pavements. You just can't imagine it, you would have to follow everyone to do any good. So we chatted for a few minutes, the blind man and I, about something or other which I've now forgotten – I'd have to check in my notebook – but I liked him. Generally, if I like someone, I don't worry, I'm sure to bump into them again. But in this case, no, nothing. Last month, I followed twenty-eight people and got close to nine of them. I filled two and a half notebooks. So I've covered a lot of ground, OK? But not a whisker of my beautiful blind man. That was disappointing. He's called Charles Reyer, and that's all I know about him. Tell me something: do you keep doodling all the time like that?'

'Yes, all the time.'

'I suppose you won't let me see.'

'No, that's right. You don't get to see.'

'It's funny when you turn round on your chair. Your left profile is tough and your right profile is tender. So if you want to intimidate a suspect, you turn one way, and when you want to soften him up, you turn the other way.'

Adamsberg smiled.

'What if I keep turning from side to side?'

'Then they won't know where they are. Heaven and hell.'

Mathilde burst out laughing. Then she controlled herself.

'No, stop,' she said again. 'I'm talking too much. I'm ashamed of myself. I've got a friend who's a philosopher, who says to me, "Mathilde, you play fast and loose with language." I said, well, in that case, tell me how to play slow and tight.'

'Look, let's see what we can do,' said Adamsberg. 'Do you have a work address?'

'You're not going to believe me. My name is Mathilde Forestier.'

Adamsberg put his pencil back in his pocket.

'Ah,' he said. 'Mathilde Forestier. Famous oceanographer. Am I right?'

'Yes, but don't let that stop you doing your doodling. I know who you are too, your name's on the door, and everyone's heard of you. But it doesn't stop me rabbiting on about one thing and another, at the end of a section one, what's more.'

'If I find your beautiful blind man, I'll tell you.'

'Why? Who would you be doing the favour for?' asked

Mathilde, suspiciously. 'For me, or for the famous underwater specialist whose name is in the papers?'

'Neither one nor the other. I'm doing a favour for a woman I asked into my office.'

'OK, that suits me,' said Mathilde. She remained for a moment without speaking, as if hesitating to take a decision. Adamsberg had brought out his cigarettes and a piece of paper. No, he wouldn't forget this woman, a fragment of the earth's beauty on the point of fading. And he was unable to guess in advance what she was going to say.

'Know something?' Mathilde asked suddenly. 'It's at nightfall that things start happening, under the ocean the same as in the city. They all start stirring, the creatures who are hungry or in pain. And the searchers, like you, Jean-Baptiste Adamsberg, they start stirring then too.'

'You think I'm searching for something?'

'Absolutely, and quite a lot of things at the same time. So, anyway, the chalk circle man comes out when he's hungry. He prowls, he watches, and suddenly he draws his circle. But I know him, I started looking for him right at the beginning, and I found him, the night there was a cigarette lighter in the circle, and the night of the doll's head. And then again, last night, in the rue Caulaincourt.'

'How did you manage that?'

'I'll tell you some other time. It's not important, it's my little secret. And it's a funny thing but you'd think he was allowing me to watch him, the chalk circle man, as if he was letting himself be tamed from a distance. If you want to see him some night, come and find me. But you must only watch him from a distance. No going up to him and bothering him. I'm not telling the famous policeman about my secret, I'm just telling the man who asked me into his office.'

'That suits me,' said Adamsberg.

'But why are you looking for the chalk circle man? He hasn't done anything wrong. Why are you so interested in him?'

Adamsberg looked at her.

'Because one day it'll get bigger. The thing in the middle of the circle, it'll get bigger. Please don't ask me how I know, I beg you, because I can't tell you. But it's inevitable.'

He shook his head, pushing back his hair from his eyes. 'Yes, it will get bigger.'

Adamsberg uncrossed his legs and began aimlessly re-organising the papers on his desk.

'I can't forbid you to follow him,' he added. 'But I really don't advise it. Be cautious, take very good care. Don't forget.'

He was uneasy, as if his own conviction made him feel unwell. Mathilde smiled and left.

Coming out of his office a little later, Adamsberg took Danglard by the shoulder and spoke quietly to him.

'Tomorrow morning, try to find out if there's been a new circle in the night. And if so, give it a thorough examination. I'm counting on you. I told that woman to watch out. This thing is going to get bigger, Danglard. There have been more circles over the last month. The rhythm's picking up. There's something horrible underneath all this, can't you feel it?'

Danglard thought for a moment, then answered with some hesitation.

'A bit unhealthy that's all. But perhaps it's just some long-drawn-out practical joke . . .'

'No, Danglard. There's cruelty oozing out of those circles.'

III

CHARLES REYER WAS ALSO JUST LEAVING HIS OFFICE. HE WAS FED up with working for the blind, checking the printing and perforations of all those wretched books in Braille, the billions of tiny holes that communicated their meaning to the skin of his fingertips. Above all, he was fed up with the desperate attempts he made to be original, on the pretext that he ought to become exceptional in some way, to distract people from his loss of sight. That was how he had behaved towards that woman the other day, now he thought of it, the warm-hearted one who had accosted him in the Café Saint-Jacques. An intelligent woman she had been, a bit eccentric perhaps, though he didn't really think so, but a kind-hearted and lively person, obviously. And what had he done? As usual, he'd begun showing off, trying to be original. To impress her by his conversation, to say out-of-the-way things, just so that a stranger would think, hey, this man may be blind, but he's certainly not ordinary.

And she'd gone along with it, the woman. She'd tried to play the game, to respond as quickly as she could to his mixture of false confidences and stupid remarks. But she had been sincere.

She'd told him about the shark, just like that, she'd been generous, sensitive, helpful, willing to look at his eyes and tell him what they really looked like. But he had been entirely taken up with the sensational effect he wanted to produce; he regularly stopped any heartfelt conversation by pretending to be a lucid and cynical thinker. No, Charles, he thought, you're going the wrong way about things. All this palaver ends up with your being unable to say whether your brain's still working or not.

And then there's your habit of walking alongside people in the street just to frighten them, to exert some kind of silly power over them, or going up to someone at a traffic light with your white stick, and saying 'Can I help you cross the road?' What's all that about? Just to embarrass other people, of course, and then to take full advantage of your untouchable status. Poor souls, they don't dare say anything, they just stand on the pavement, feeling bad. What you're doing is you're taking revenge on the rest of the world. You may be over six feet tall, but you're just a mean little bastard really. And that woman, Queen Mathilde, she's there, she's real, and she even told me I was good-looking. And that made me feel pretty good, but of course I couldn't bring myself to show it, or even say thank you for her kind word.

Feeling his way, Charles stopped at the edge of the pavement. Anyone standing alongside him would have been able to see those rolls of sacking that they put in the Paris gutters to channel the water, without realising how lucky they were to witness this sublime sight. Damn that bloody lioness. He felt like unfolding his white stick and asking 'Shall I help you across the road?' with a mean smile. Then he remembered Mathilde saying to him without any malice at all: 'You're *very* trying', and he turned his back on whoever might be there.

IV

Danglard had tried to resist. But the next day he fell eagerly on the newspapers, leaving aside the political, economic and social news, all the stuff that usually interested him.

No, nothing. Nothing about the chalk circle man. Not that there was anything about these incidents to merit the daily attentions of a journalist.

But now he was hooked.

The night before, his daughter, the elder of the second set of twins, the one who was most interested in what her father told her about his work – although she also said to him, 'Dad, stop drinking, you're already fat enough as it is' – had remarked: 'Your new boss has a funny name, doesn't he? Jean-Baptiste Adamsberg, Saint John the Baptist from Adam's Mountain, if you work it out. Looks funny when you put it together. But if you like him, I expect I'll like him. Will you take me to see him one day?' And Danglard loved his four twins so much that he would have wished above all to show *them* to Adamsberg, so that his boss could say 'They're angelic.' But he wasn't sure whether Adamsberg would be interested in his kids. 'My kids, my kids, my kids,' Danglard said to himself. 'My angels.'

From his office, he called all the district police stations to find out whether any officer on the beat had noticed a circle. 'Just asking, since everyone's got interested in it.' His questions provoked astonishment. He explained that it was on behalf of a psychiatrist friend, a little favour he was doing him on the side. And yes, of course, his fellow cops knew all about the little favours one did for people on the side.

And last night, it turned out, Paris had acquired two new circles. The first was in the rue du Moulin-Vert, where a policeman from the 14th *arrondissement* had come across it on his rounds, to his great delight. The other was in the same district, on the corner of the rue Froidevaux, and it had been reported by a woman who had complained to the police that she thought this was getting a bit much.

Danglard, feeling on edge and impatient, went upstairs to see Conti, the police photographer. Conti was all set to go, laden with straps and containers, as if on campaign. Since the photographer suffered from various health problems, Danglard imagined that all this complicated and impressive technical stuff must provide him with some kind of reassurance, although he knew perfectly well that Conti wasn't stupid. They went first to the rue du Moulin-Vert, and there was the large circle, drawn in blue chalk, with the same elegant writing round the edge. Lying slightly off-centre was part of a watch strap. Why draw such big circles for such small objects, Danglard wondered. Until now he hadn't thought about this discrepancy.

'Don't touch!' he shouted to Conti, who had stepped into the circle to take a closer look.

'What are you fussing about?' said Conti. 'This strap hasn't been murdered. Call the pathologist while you're at it!'

The photographer shrugged and stepped back out of the circle.

'Don't ask questions,' said Danglard. 'He said to take pictures of it exactly as it is, so please just do that.'

While Conti was snapping away, Danglard reflected all the same that Adamsberg had put him in a slightly ridiculous situation. If any local policeman should come past, he'd be right to say that the 5th *arrondissement* station was going round the bend if it had taken to photographing watch straps. And Danglard did feel that the 5th was indeed heading round the bend, himself along with the rest. What was more, he still hadn't tied up everything on the Patrice Vernoux case, which he ought to have done first thing. His colleague Castreau was probably wondering by now where he'd got to.

In the rue Froidevaux, at the junction with the rue Emile-Richard, the lugubrious and narrow passage running through the middle of the Montparnasse cemetery, Danglard understood why the woman had complained, and was almost relieved to discover the reason.

Yes, it had got bigger.

'See that?' he said to Conti.

In front of them, the blue circle surrounded the remains of a cat that had been run over. There was no blood: the cat had obviously been picked out of the gutter where it had been dead for hours. Now it just looked morbid, a bundle of dirty fur in this sinister street, with the circle and the inscription '*Victor, woe's in store, what are you out here for?*' It made him think of some kind of weird witches' spell.

'All finished,' said Conti.

Stupid, perhaps, but Danglard sensed that Conti was a bit impressed.

'I've finished too,' said Danglard. 'Come on, back to base before the locals find us on their patch.'

'Yeah, right,' said Conti. 'We'd look pretty silly.'

Adamsberg listened to Danglard's report impassively, allowing his cigarette to droop from his lips, screwing up his eyes to keep the smoke out of them. The only movement he made throughout was to bite off a piece of fingernail. And as Danglard was beginning to get the measure of his character, he realised that Adamsberg had assessed the discovery in the rue Froidevaux at its true value.

But what was that, exactly? For the moment, Danglard had no idea. The way Adamsberg's mind worked was still enigmatic and impressive to him. Sometimes, but only for a second, he thought: Keep your distance.

But he knew the moment the report went round the station that the boss was wasting his own and his inspectors' time on the chalk circle man, Danglard would have to defend him. And he was trying to prepare his defence.

'Yesterday a mouse,' said Danglard, as if talking to himself, practising future explanations to his colleagues. 'And now a cat. It's a bit nasty, yes. But there was the watch strap as well. And as Conti rightly pointed out, the watch strap wasn't dead.'

'It was dead all right,' said Adamsberg. 'Of course it was! Same thing tomorrow morning, Danglard. I'm going to see this psychiatrist who's taken up the affair, Vercors-Laury. I'd be interested to hear what he thinks. But don't tell anyone. The later anyone asks what I'm up to, the better.'

Before leaving, Adamsberg wrote a note for Mathilde Forestier. It had taken him less than an hour to track down her Charles Reyer, after telephoning the main organisations that employed blind people in Paris: piano tuners, publishing houses, music schools. Reyer had been in the city several months, and was staying in a room near the Pantheon, at the Hôtel des Grands Hommes. Adamsberg sent the information to Mathilde, and promptly forgot about it.

Well, René Vercors-Laury isn't all that impressive, was Adamsberg's first reaction. He was disappointed in the psychiatrist, since he always set out feeling hopeful and disillusion was invariably painful.

Not impressive at all, in fact. And exasperating with it. The psychiatrist kept interrupting himself with questions like: 'See what I mean?', 'You follow me?' or statements such as: 'You'll agree with me, won't you, that the Socratic method of suicide is not the only model?' – without waiting for Adamsberg's reply, since the intention was simply to show off. Vercors-Laury expended an inordinate amount of time and words showing off. The portly doctor would first lean back in his armchair, fingers clutching his belt, seeming to think deeply, and would then hurl himself forward to begin a sentence: '*Commissaire*, this is no ordinary case.'

If one set all that aside, the man wasn't lacking in intelligence; that much at least was clear. After the first quarter of an hour, things went better; still not impressive, perhaps, but better.

'Our subject,' said Vercors-Laury, launching into a peroration, 'does not fit the normal pattern of subjects with a compulsive disorder, if you are asking for my clinical opinion.

Compulsives are by definition *compulsive*, and one should never forget that – do you follow me?'

He was clearly highly satisfied with this formula. He went on:

'And because they are compulsive, obsessive, they're precise, careful, and ritualistic. You follow me? But what do we find with this subject? No ritual governing the choice of object, no ritual governing the choice of district, or the time of night, or even the number of circles to draw on any given night. So! You see the immense discrepancy? All the parameters of his actions vary unpredictably: object, place, time, quantity, as if they were entirely determined by chance circumstance. But, *Commissaire* Adamsberg, in the case of a compulsive personality *nothing* is determined by chance circumstance. Are you with me? And that is, in point of fact, the defining feature of the compulsive subject: he will make the chance circumstance bend to his will, rather than allow it to drive him. No contingency is strong enough to halt the relentless progress of his obsession. You see what I'm driving at?'

'So what we have here is no common-or-garden crank? Not a compulsive personality at all?'

'That's right, *commissaire*, we could almost swear to it. And that opens up a whole field of inquiry. If we're not dealing with an obsessive-compulsive personality in the clinical sense of the term, then the circles must be in pursuit of some aim which has been thoroughly thought through by their perpetrator, and our subject must have a genuine interest in the objects that he's bringing to our attention, as if he meant to show us something. You follow me? Or to tell us something. For instance, that people don't think enough about the objects they throw away. Once these objects have ceased to be useful, once they have served their purpose, our eyes don't even see them as material any more. I could show you a pavement and say: "What do you see on the ground?" and you could reply: "Nothing." Whereas *in reality*' (heavy emphasis) 'there are dozens of objects there. You follow? This man appears to be grappling with a painful investigation of some kind: metaphysical, philosophical, or perhaps – why not? – poetic, about the way human beings choose to make the reality of the material world start and stop, something for which he has elected himself the arbiter. Whereas in *his* eyes, it may be that material objects continue their existence outside our perception of them. My sole aim, when I took an interest in this man, was to say: Take care, don't joke about this obsessive behaviour pattern, the chalk circle man may be someone of perfectly lucid mind, who cannot express himself except through these manifestations, which are, indeed, evidence of a mind in *some* sense deranged, yet at the same time highly organised, you follow? But someone of above average intelligence, believe me.'

'But there are mistakes in the series. The mouse and then the cat, they weren't objects.'

'As I said, there's much less logic to the series than might appear at first, the kind of logic we would find if this were a case of authentic obsession. That's what's so unsettling about it. But from the point of view of our subject, he is demonstrating that death transforms a living creature into an object the moment the lifeless body ceases to feel anything – which is true enough. From the instant the top comes off the bottle, the top becomes a non-thing. And when the body of a friend stops breathing – what does it become? Our man is preoccupied with questions of this order. In fact, not to put too fine a point on it: he's obsessed with death.'

Vercors-Laury paused, leaning back once more in his chair. He looked Adamsberg straight in the eye, as if to say: Listen carefully, I'm about to tell you something sensational. Adamsberg did not believe he would do anything of the sort.

'From your point of view as a policeman, you are wondering whether he poses any danger to human life, aren't you, *commissaire*? I'll tell you this much: the phenomenon could remain stable at this stage and burn itself out, but on the other hand I see no reason why, *theoretically*, a man of this kind, in other words a deranged person who is nevertheless perfectly in control of himself (if you have followed me so far), a man burning with the need to exhibit his thoughts, should halt in his trajectory. Note that I'm saying *theoretically*.'

Adamsberg walked back to the office with vague thoughts running through his head. He was not in the habit of reflecting deeply. He had never been able to understand what was happening when he saw people put their hands to their foreheads and say, 'Right, let's give this some thought.' What was going on in their brains, the way they managed to organise precise ideas, inferring, deducting, concluding, all that was a complete mystery to him. He had to admit that it produced undeniable results, and that after this kind of brainstorming, people took decisions, something he admired while being convinced that he was himself lacking in some way. But when he tried it, when he sat down and said 'Right, I'll give it some thought,' nothing happened in his head. It was even at moments like that that he was aware of a complete blank.

Adamsberg never realised when he was thinking and the instant he became conscious of it, it stopped. As a result he was never sure where all his ideas, his intentions and his decisions came from.

At any rate, he felt that nothing that Vercors-Laury had said had come as a surprise, and that he had always known that the man drawing the blue chalk circles was no ordinary crackpot. That some cruel motive lay underneath this apparent lunacy. That the sequence of objects could only lead to one conclusion, one blinding apotheosis: a death. Mathilde Forestier would have said that it was normal not to learn anything serious, since it was the second section of the week, but Adamsberg thought it was simply that Vercors-Laury was someone who knew his stuff all right, but wasn't in the end all that impressive.

The following morning, a large blue circle had appeared in the rue Cunin-Gridaine in the 3rd *arrondissement*. The only thing in the centre was a hairpin.

Conti photographed the hairpin.

The next night brought a circle in the rue Lacretelle and another in the rue de la Condamine, in the 17th *arrondissement*, one containing an old handbag, the other a cotton bud.

Conti photographed the bag and then the cotton bud, without passing comment, but the look on his face betrayed his irritation. Danglard remained silent.

The next three nights produced a one-franc coin, a torch battery, a screwdriver, and something which cheered Danglard up somewhat, if that was the right expression, a dead pigeon with one wing torn off, in the rue Geoffroy-Saint-Hilaire.

Disconcertingly, Adamsberg showed no reaction except a

vague smile. He was still cutting out any newspaper articles that mentioned the chalk circle man and stuffing them into his desk drawer, alongside the photographs supplied by Conti. By now, everyone in the station knew about it, and Danglard was becoming rather anxious on his behalf. But the full confession obtained from Patrice Vernoux had made Adamsberg untouchable, at least for a little while.

'How long is this business going to go on, *commissaire*?' asked Danglard.

'What business?'

'The chalk circles, for Christ's sake! We're not going to stand in front of these damned hairpins every morning for the rest of our lives, are we?'

'Ah, the chalk circles. Yes, it could go on a long time, Danglard. A very long time, even. But so what? Whether we follow this or do something else, does it matter? Hairpins provide a bit of distraction.'

'So we drop the whole thing?'

Adamsberg looked up abruptly.

'Absolutely not, Danglard, out of the question.'

'You can't be serious.'

'As serious as I can be. It's going to get bigger, Danglard, as I've already told you.'

Danglard shrugged.

'We'll need all this documentation,' Adamsberg went on, opening the drawer. 'It could be indispensable afterwards.'

'After what, for God's sake?'

'Don't get impatient, Danglard – you wouldn't wish someone dead, would you?'

Next morning there was an ice-cream cone in the avenue du Docteur-Brouardel in the 7th *arrondissement*.

V

Mathilde had presented herself at the Hôtel Des Grands Hommes, to look for the beautiful blind man – a very small hotel for such a grand name, she thought. Or perhaps it meant that one didn't need many rooms to accommodate all the great men in the world.

The receptionist, after telephoning to announce her arrival, told her that Monsieur Reyer couldn't come down, he was detained. Mathilde went up to his room.

'What's the matter?' Mathilde cried through the locked door. 'Are you naked in bed with someone?'

'No,' said Charles.

'Something more serious?'

'I'm not looking my best. I can't find my razor.'

Mathilde thought for a moment. 'It's out of sight, you mean?'

'Yes, right,' said Charles. 'I've felt everywhere. I don't understand.'

He opened the door.

'You have to appreciate, Queen Mathilde, that things take advantage of my weakness. I hate *things*. They disguise themselves, they slip between the mattress and the bed, they knock over the waste-paper basket, they get stuck between the floorboards. I've had enough. I think I'm going to abolish things.'

'You're not as smart as a fish,' Mathilde observed. 'Because the fish that live right down on the seabed, in complete darkness, like you, they manage to find what they want to eat, in spite of everything.'

'Fish don't have to shave. And anyway, what the eye doesn't see the heart doesn't grieve after. Couldn't give a damn about your fish.'

'Eyes, eyes. You're doing it on purpose aren't you?'

'Yes, I am doing it on purpose, I've got a whole repertoire of expressions: I'll cast my eye over it, I'll make eyes at her, I've got my eye on you, I'll keep my eyes peeled, it's an eye-opener, I've got eyes in the back of my head. There are plenty of them. I like using them. Like other people like to chew over their memories. But anyway, I really couldn't care less about fish.'

'Plenty of people feel like that. Yes, it's true, there's a general tendency not to give a damn about fish. Can I sit on this chair?'

'Please go ahead. Anyway, what's so marvellous about fish?'

'We understand each other, me and the fish. We've spent thirty years in each other's company now, so we don't dare leave each other. If I was dumped by a fish, I'd be lost. The fish are my work, they produce my income, they keep me if you like.'

'And because I'm like one of your damned fish swimming about in the dark, that's why you've come to see me.'

Mathilde thought for a moment.

'You won't get anywhere like that,' she concluded. 'You need to be a bit more fishy, that's exactly it – more flexible and fluid. Still, it's up to you if you want to make the whole universe feel guilty. I came because you said you were looking for a flat, and it looks as if you're still needing one. Perhaps you don't have a lot of money. This hotel's a bit dear, though.'

'The ghosts that haunt it are dear to me too. But the main thing, Queen Mathilde, is that people don't want to rent rooms to a blind man. They're afraid that the blind man will do stupid things: drop his plate over the side of the table, piss all over the carpet because he thinks he's in the bathroom.'

'Well, a blind man would suit me fine. All my work on the three-spined stickleback, the flying gurnard and the sawback angelshark has paid for three apartments, in the same house, on three different floors. I had a big family living on the first and third floors – the Sawback Angelshark flat and the Three-Spined Stickleback flat, I call them – but they've moved out. I live on the second floor, named after the Flying Gurnard. I've rented the Stickleback out to an eccentric old lady, and I thought of you as a possible tenant for the Sawback Angelshark – call it the first floor if you like. I won't charge you a high rent.'

'Why not?'

Charles heard Mathilde laugh and light a cigarette. He groped for an ashtray, which he held out to her.

'You're offering the ashtray to the window,' said Mathilde. 'I'm sitting a good metre to the left of where you think.'

'My apologies. You're a hard woman, aren't you? Most people would stretch out their hand to take the ashtray and wouldn't pass remarks.'

'You'll find I'm even harder when you discover that the

apartment is fine and a good size, but people don't like living there because they find it too dark. So I said to myself: now Charles Reyer, that's someone I like. And since he's blind, it'll suit him down to the ground, because what difference will it make to him if the flat's dark?'

'Are you always this tactless?' Charles asked.

'Yes, I think so,' replied Mathilde, seriously. 'Anyway, what about the Angelshark – does it tempt you?'

'I'd like to take a good look,' said Charles, with a smile, twitching his glasses. 'I think it might suit me very well, a dark angelshark. But if I'm going to live there I'll need to know the habits of this sea creature, otherwise my own apartment will think I'm an idiot.'

'Easy. The *Squatina aculeata*, or sawback angelshark, sometimes known as the monkfish, is migratory, and frequents the shallow coastal shelves of the Mediterranean. Its flesh is rather bland, some people like it, others don't. It swims like a shark, propelling itself with its tail. It has a snub nose and fringed nasal barbels. Its gills are large and half-moon in shape, its mouth is armed with unicuspid teeth on a wide base – and so on and so forth. It's brown with dark speckles and pale spots, a bit like the carpet in the hall.'

'I could learn to like a creature like that, Queen Mathilde.'

It was seven o'clock. Clémence Valmont was working in Mathilde's flat. She was classifying slides and felt unbearably hot. She would have liked to take off her black beret, she would have liked not to be seventy years old, and for her hair not to be thinning on top. These days she never took off her beret. This evening she would show Mathilde two small ads from the day's paper, which were quite interesting and to which she was tempted to reply.

M., 66, well-preserved, large appetite, small pension, would like to meet F., not too ugly, small appetite, large pension, to keep each other company on the last stretch of the road.

Well, at least that was frank. And the next one was pretty irresistible:

Successful Medium and Clairvoyant with Gift inherited from Father The whole truth from first meeting whether for protection lasting affection tracing lost husband or wife attraction happiness consultation by correspondence send photo and SAE for entire satisfaction in every domain.

What have I got to lose? said Clémence to herself.

The Sawback Angelshark flat had pleased Charles Reyer. He had already made up his mind, in fact, when Mathilde had told him about it in the hotel, and he had merely concealed his haste to accept. Because Charles knew that he was getting worse, month by month. And he was afraid. He sensed that Mathilde, without even realising it, would be able to distract his mind from the dark and morbid sentiments into which it was sinking. At the same time, he could see no other solution than to keep hating everybody, since the idea of becoming a sort of Pollyanna blind man revolted him. He had gone round the walls of the apartment, feeling with his hands, and Mathilde had shown him where the doors, taps and light switches were.

'Why bother showing me the light switches?' said Charles. 'No need to put the light on. You're not as clever as you think, Queen Mathilde.'

Mathilde shrugged. She realised that Charles Reyer turned nasty about every ten minutes.

'What about other people?' she replied. 'If someone comes to see you, you won't put the light on, will you, just let them sit in the dark?'

'Hate other people, feel like killing them,' said Charles through clenched teeth, as if to excuse himself.

He cast about for a chair, bumped into the unfamiliar furniture and Mathilde did not help him. So he remained standing and turned towards her.

'Am I more or less facing you?'

'More or less.'

'Put the light on, Mathilde.'

'It is on.'

Charles took off his glasses and Mathilde looked at his eyes.

'Well, obviously,' she said after a moment. 'Don't expect me to tell you your eyes look fine, because they don't, they're horrible. Against your pale skin, frankly they make you look like the living dead. With your glasses on, you're terrific. But when you take them off, you look like a scorpion-fish. If I was a surgeon, my dear Charles, I'd try and fix them for you, clean them up. There's no reason why you should carry on looking like a scorpion-fish if there's a way out. I know someone, a surgeon. He did a great job on a friend who'd had an accident that left him with a face like a John Dory. The John Dory's not a pretty fish either.'

'What if I *like* looking like a scorpion-fish?' asked Charles.

'Dear God,' said Mathilde. 'Are you going to plague me for the rest of my days moaning about being blind? You want to look terrible? OK, go ahead, look terrible. You want to go on being mean and nasty, making cutting remarks that reduce other people to shreds ? All right, go ahead, my dear Charles, see if it bothers me. You won't know about this yet, but you're out of luck, because it's Thursday today. So we're at the start of a section two of the week, and until Sunday, inclusive, I will have absolutely no moral sense. You want compassion, a sympathetic ear, insight, encouragement, or any other humanitarian sentiments, sorry, that's all over for this week. We get born, we die, and in between we destroy ourselves wasting time while we pretend to be spending it productively, and that's all I want to say just now about the human race. Next Monday, I shall find humanity perfectly splendid with all its foibles and procrastinations, as it slouches towards the millennium. But today, nothing doing, the office is closed. Today's a day for cynicism, *laissez-aller*, futility, and immediate gratification. If you want to look like a scorpion-fish, or a moray eel, or a gargoyle or a two-headed hydra, or a teratomorph, well, feel free, Charles, go ahead. You won't upset me. I like all the fish in the sea, even disgusting fish, so this isn't a conversation for a Thursday at all. You're unsettling my week, carrying on like this with your hysterical revenge. See, what *would* have been a good thing to do in a section two of the week, would be to go upstairs and have a drink in the Flying Gurnard, where I could have introduced you to the old lady who lives on the top floor. But today, no, out of the question, you'd be too nasty to her. You have to treat Clémence with kid gloves. Seventy years old and she's just got one idea in her head, to find the love of her life, and a man, hopefully at the same time, which is a tall order. You see, Charles, everyone has their own troubles. She's got plenty of love to give, she falls for every lonely-heart announcement in the paper. She looks through all the small ads, she replies to them, she goes along for a date, she's invariably humiliated, so she comes back home and starts again. To tell you the truth, I think she's a bit soft in the head, desperately nice, always trying to help, and pulling packs of cards out of the pockets of her baggy old trousers to tell people's fortunes. And I'll tell you what she looks like, since you have this silly habit of not seeing: she's not very attractive, she's got a bony, rather masculine face, with sharp little teeth like a shrew-mouse, *Crocidura russula*, you wouldn't want to get your hand caught by them. And she wears far too much make-up. I hire her two days a week to file my papers and slides. She's very precise and patient, as if she was never going to die, and sometimes I find that restful. She works away with her mind on other things, whispering about her dreams and her pathetic adventures, going over the hypothetical meetings with Mr Right, preparing what to say to the next one, and despite all that she's very good at filing, although like you she couldn't care less about fish. That's the only thing you might have in common.'

'So you think we'll get on?' asked Charles.

'Don't worry, you'll hardly ever see her. She's always trotting off somewhere looking for the future husband. And as for you, you don't love anyone, so as my mother would say, what's the rush?'

'True,' said Charles.

VI

THE FOLLOWING THURSDAY MORNING TWO CIRCLES WERE discovered: in the rue de l'Abbé-de-l'Epée was the cork from a wine bottle, and in the rue Pierre-et-Marie-Curie, in the 5th *arrondissement*, lay a woman with her throat cut, staring up at the sky.

In spite of the shock, Adamsberg could not help thinking that the discovery had been made at the beginning of section two of the week, the time for unimportant things, but that the murder must have been committed at the end of the first section, the serious one.

He paced around his office, with a less vague expression than usual on his face, his chin thrust forward, his mouth open as if he was out of breath. Danglard saw that Adamsberg was preoccupied, but that he nevertheless didn't give the impression of deep concentration. Their previous *commissaire* had been just the opposite. He had been completely tied up in his thoughts, a man of perpetual rumination. But Adamsberg was open to every wind, like a cabin made of rough planks, letting his brain receive fresh air, Danglard thought. Yes, it was true, you could imagine that everything that went in through his ears, eyes and nose – smoke, colours, paper rustling – caused a draught to whistle through his thoughts and stopped them solidifying. This man, thought Danglard, is attentive to everything, which means he pays attention to nothing. The four inspectors were even getting into the habit of walking in and out of his office without fear of interrupting any particular train of thought. And Danglard had noticed that at certain times Adamsberg was more absent-minded than at others. When he was doodling, not resting his notepad on his knee but holding a little piece of paper against his stomach, then Danglard would say to himself: If I were to announce to him now that a giant fungus was about to engulf the Earth and squeeze it to the size of a grapefruit, he wouldn't give a damn. And that would be a pretty serious matter – not room for many people on a grapefruit. As anyone can see.'

Florence was also watching the *commissaire*. Since her conversation with Castreau she had thought again, and had announced that the new *commissaire* made her think of a rather depraved Florentine prince she had seen in a picture in some book, but now she couldn't remember which. Anyway, she would like to sit on a bench and look at him as if he were a picture in an exhibition when she'd had enough of life, enough of finding ladders in her tights, and enough of hearing Danglard tell her he didn't know when the universe would come to an end, or indeed why it was the universe anyway.

She watched them drive off in two cars to the rue Pierre-et-Marie-Curie.

In the car, Danglard muttered: 'A cork and a woman with her throat cut. Can't see the connection – it's beyond me. I don't understand what's going through this character's mind.'

'If you look at water in a bucket,' Adamsberg said, 'you

can see the bottom of the bucket. You can put your arm in, you can touch it. Or even a barrel, same thing. But if it's a well, there's no hope. Even if you chuck pebbles in to see how deep it is, it's no use. Problem is, you keep on trying to understand. People always want to "understand". And that way madness lies. You wouldn't believe the number of little pebbles there are at the bottom of a well. It's not to hear the splash that people throw them, really. No, it's to under-stand. But a well is a terrible thing. Once the people who built them have died, nobody knows anything about the well. It's beyond our reach, it's laughing at us from deep inside its mysterious cylindrical belly, full of water. That's what a well's like, for me. But how much water is there? How deep does it go? You have to lean over, to find out, you have to lower ropes down inside it.'

'You can get drowned like that,' said Castreau.

'Yes, of course.'

'I don't see what this has to do with the murder,' said Castreau.

'I didn't say it had anything to do with it,' said Adamsberg.

'Then why did you get us started on wells?'

'Why not? The things we talk about don't always have to be relevant. But Danglard's right. There doesn't seem to be any connection between a wine cork and a dead woman. But that's exactly what's important.'

The eyes of the murdered woman were open, with a terri-fied expression in them, and her mouth was open too, her jaw virtually dislocated. It almost looked as if she had been shouting the rhyme which was written all round the circle surrounding her: '*Victor, woe's in store, what are you out here for?*'

The sound was deafening, enough to make one want to stop one's ears, and yet the policemen standing in a group around the circle were silent.

Danglard was looking at the woman's cheap raincoat, buttoned up tightly, at her throat which had been cut, and at the blood which had trickled as far as the door of a building. He felt sick. He had never been able to view a corpse without feeling sick, something which did not however distress him. It wasn't unpleasant to feel sick. It made him forget his other sorrows, the sorrows of the soul, he thought bitterly.

'She was killed by a rat, a human rat,' said Adamsberg. 'Rats leap at people's throats like that.'

Then he added.

'So who is this lady?'

His *petite chérie* always said 'lady' and 'gentleman'. 'That's a pretty lady.' 'That gentleman wants to go to bed with me', and Adamsberg hadn't been able to rid himself of the habit.

Inspecteur Delille replied:

'Her papers were on the body – the murderer didn't take anything. Her name was Madeleine Châtelain, aged fifty-one.'

'Have you searched her bag?'

'Not thoroughly, but it doesn't look as if there's anything out of the ordinary.'

'Tell me all the same.'

'A knitting magazine, a tiny penknife, some of those little soaps you get in hotels, her wallet and keys, a pink plastic eraser and a pocket diary.'

'Anything in the diary for yesterday?'

'Yes, but not a rendezvous, if that's what you were hoping. She'd written "It's not much fun working in a knitting shop."'

'Any other entries like that?'

'Quite a few. Three days ago, for instance: "God knows why Maman's so keen on dry Martinis." And the week before that: "Nothing could *ever* persuade me to go to the top of the Eiffel Tower."'

Adamsberg smiled. The police pathologist was muttering that you couldn't expect miracles if bodies weren't discovered quickly enough, that he thought she had probably been killed between ten-thirty and midnight, but that he would prefer to check the stomach contents before stating anything with confidence. The knife wound had been made with a medium-sized blade, following a massive blow to the head.

Adamsberg stopped thinking about the little entries in the diary and looked at Danglard. The inspector was pale and gave the impression of being on the point of collapse, his arms dangling at the sides of his shapeless body. He was also frowning.

'You've seen what's wrong?' asked Adamsberg.

'I'm not sure. What bothers me is that the trail of blood has run over the chalk circle and covered quite a bit of it.'

'Yes, exactly, Danglard. And the lady's hand is right up against the line. If he drew the circle after killing her, the chalk might have made a channel through the blood. And if I had been the murderer, I think I would have gone wider around the body to draw the circle. I don't think I would have gone so close to her hand.'

'So it's as if the circle was drawn first, is that what you mean? And then the murderer arranged the body inside it?'

'Looks a bit like that. But that seems stupid, doesn't it? Danglard, would you go and check all this out with the scene-of-crime people and with the graphologist – Meunier, I think he's called. This is where Conti's photos are going to help us, and so will the dimensions of all the previous circles and the chalk samples you collected. We'll have to compare them all with this new circle. We have to find out whether it's the same man who drew it, and whether he drew it before or after the murder. Delille, can you follow up this lady's address, her neighbours, friends and contacts? Castreau, check her place of work, if she had one, who her colleagues were, and what her income was. Nivelle, you take the family side of things, any family quarrels, inheritances, love affairs.'

Adamsberg had spoken without haste. It was the first time Danglard had seen him giving orders. He did so without seeming either self-important or apologetic about doing so. It was an odd thing, but all the inspectors seemed to be becoming porous, letting Adamsberg's way of behaving seep into them. It was like being caught in the rain when your jacket can't help absorbing water. The inspectors were becoming damp and without realising it they were imitating Adamsberg; their movements were slower, they smiled more, and were absent-minded. The one most altered was Castreau, who as a rule liked the gruff, manly responses their previous *commissaire* had expected of them, the military commands barked out without any superfluous commentary, the ban on looking to either side, the slamming of car doors, the fists clenched in the tunic pockets. Today, Danglard hardly recognised Castreau. He was leafing through the victim's pocket diary, quietly reading out sentences to himself, glancing attentively at Adamsberg, apparently considering every word, and Danglard thought to himself that he might be able to confess to him his problems about corpses.

'If I go on looking at her, I'll be sick,' Danglard said to Castreau.

'It gets me in the knees. Especially women, even women like this one, nothing much to look at.'

'What are you reading in the diary?'

'Listen: "Had a perm, but I'm still ugly. Papa was ugly, so was Maman. Why would I be any different? A customer came in for blue mohair but I didn't have any left. Another bad day."'

Adamsberg watched the four inspectors get back in the car. He was thinking about his *petite chérie*, Richard III and the lady's diary. Once the *petite chérie* had asked him: 'Is a murder like a packet of spaghetti that's all stuck together? You just have to put it in boiling water for it to come untangled again? And the boiling water's the motive?' and he had replied: 'No, what gets it untangled is knowledge, you just have to let the knowledge come to you.' She had said: 'I'm not sure I understood that', which was fair enough, since he didn't really understand it himself.

He waited for the police doctor, who was still grumbling away, to finish his preliminary check of the body. The photographer and the scene-of-crime people had already left. He stood alone, looking down at the lady on the ground, with the stretcher team waiting nearby. He hoped that a little knowledge would come to him. But until he came face to face with the chalk circle man, he knew it wasn't worth racking his brains. He just had to keep on picking up information, and for him information had nothing to do with knowledge.

VII

Since Charles seemed to be feeling better about things, Mathilde decided that she could count on a peaceful quarter of an hour during which he wouldn't try to reduce the universe to shreds, and that she would therefore be able to introduce him to Clémence that evening. She had asked the elderly Clémence to stay behind in the flat for the occasion, and had taken some pre-emptive action by warning her emphatically that the new tenant was indeed blind, but that it would not do either to exclaim, 'Oh my sakes, what a terrible affliction!' or to pretend complete ignorance.

Charles heard Mathilde introduce him and listened to Clémence's greeting. From her voice, he would never have imagined the naive woman whom Queen Mathilde had described to him. He seemed to hear fierce determination, and weird but recognisable intelligence. What she actually said seemed silly, but in the intonations behind the words there was some secret knowledge, caged but breathing audibly, like a lion in a village circus. You hear it growling in the night and tell yourself this circus isn't what you thought, it isn't quite as pathetic as the programme might make you think.

And Charles, the expert on sounds and noises, could quite distinctly hear this distant growling, a little unsettling since it was possibly concealed.

Mathilde had offered him a whisky and Clémence was telling him about the incidents in her life. Charles was troubled, because of Clémence, and happy because of Mathilde. A divine creature who was quite indifferent to his nastiness.

'. . . and this man,' Clémence was saying, 'anyone would think he was really nice! He thought I was "interesting", those were his very words. He never so much as touched me, but I guessed he would sooner or later. Because he wanted to take me on a trip to the South Seas, he wanted us to get married. Oh, my sakes, I was on cloud nine! He got me to sell my house in Neuilly, and my furniture. I put the rest of my things in two suitcases, because he said "You won't want for *any*thing, my dear." So I trotted along to our rendezvous in Paris, feeling so happy that I should have smelled a rat. I kept pinching myself and saying, "Clémence, old girl, it was a long time coming, but it's happened at last, a real fiancé, and such a cultured man too, and now you're going to see the Pacific." Well, I didn't see the Pacific, monsieur, I saw Censier-Daubenton metro station for eight and a half hours! I waited all day, and that's where Mathilde found me, still at the metro station, in the evening, same place she'd seen me in the morning. She must have said to herself, my sakes, but something's up with *that* old woman. Perhaps she's jinxed.'

'Clémence invents things, you know,' Mathilde interrupted. 'She reruns anything she doesn't like. What really happened the night this famous fiancé stood her up at Censier-Daubenton was that in the end she went off to find a hotel, and going along my street she saw my "to let" sign. So she rang the bell.'

'Well, maybe it could have happened that way,' Clémence conceded. 'But now I can't take the metro at Censier-Daubenton, without thinking of the South Sea Islands. So there we are, I go travelling in the end. By the way, Mathilde, a gentleman telephoned twice for you. Very soft voice, I thought I'd *faint* listening to him, but I've forgotten his name. It was urgent, apparently. Something wrong.'

Clémence was always on the brink of fainting, but she might be right about the voice on the phone. Mathilde thought that it could have been that policeman, the half-weird, half-enchanting one she had met ten days earlier. But she could think of no reason why Jean-Baptiste Adamsberg should call her urgently. Unless he had remembered her offer to help him catch sight of the chalk circle man. She had proposed that on an impulse, but also because she would be sorry never to have an excuse in future to see this remarkable *flic*, who had been the real find of that day and who had saved the first section of her week at the last moment. She knew she would not easily forget him, that he was securely lodged somewhere in her memory, spreading his nonchalant luminosity. Mathilde found the number that Clémence had scribbled down in her cramped handwriting.

Adamsberg had gone home to wait for a call from Mathilde Forestier. The day had started out typical of the aftermath of a murder, a day of silent, sweaty activity by the lab technicians, of stuffy offices with plastic cups all over the tables. The graphologist had arrived and had started delving into the piles of snapshots taken by Conti. And over it all loomed a sort of trembling, of apprehension perhaps, into which this out-of-the-ordinary event had thrown the 5th *arrondissement* police station. Whether it was the apprehension of failure, or the apprehension of a weird and monstrous killer, Adamsberg had not tried to work out. To escape having to witness it all, he had gone for a walk in the streets all afternoon. Danglard had stopped him at the door. It wasn't yet midday, but Danglard had already had too much to drink. He said it was irresponsible to walk out like that, on the day they'd had a murder. But Adamsberg couldn't admit that nothing removed his powers of thought so effectively as watching a dozen other people thinking. He needed the temperature at the station to drop, it was probably an undulant fever anyway, and it was essential that nobody should be expecting anything from him for Adamsberg to be able to harness his own ideas. And for the moment the suppressed excitement in the police station had scattered his ideas all over the place, like panicking soldiers in the thick of the battle. Adamsberg had long ago noted that when there are no combatants left, the fighting stops, so when he had no ideas he stopped working and didn't try to winkle them out of the cracks to which they had retreated. It had always turned out to be a waste of time.

Christiane was waiting at his front door.

Just his bad luck. This was one evening when he would have preferred to be alone. Or else perhaps to spend the night with his neighbour, a young woman whom he had met several times on the stair and once at the post office, and who was definitely appealing.

Christiane announced that she had come from Orleans to spend the weekend with him.

He was wondering whether the young neighbour, when

she had given him that look at the post office, had meant 'I'd like to go to bed with you' or 'I'd like a chat, I'm bored.' Adamsberg was a docile man. He tended to go to bed with any girl who wanted to: sometimes that seemed exactly the right thing to do, since it apparently kept everyone happy, other times it seemed pointless. But in any case, there was no way of knowing what it was that the girl downstairs had wanted to convey to him. He had tried thinking about that, but had put it off until later. What would his youngest sister have said? His little sister was a powerhouse of thought, enough to drive him mad. She gave her opinion of any girl-friend of his she met. Of Christiane, her judgement had been: 'B minus. Lovely body, very entertaining for an hour, medium-serious brain, centripetal mind with concentric thoughts, three key ideas, gets bored after a couple of hours, goes to bed, is extremely self-denying and biddable in love, same again next day. Overall verdict: don't get hooked, move on if a better prospect turns up.'

But that wasn't why Adamsberg wanted to avoid Christiane that evening. Perhaps it was because of the look that girl in the post office had given him. Perhaps it was simply because he had found Christiane waiting for him, so sure that he would smile when he saw her, so sure that he would open the door, and then unbutton his shirt, and then turn down the sheets, and so sure that she would be making the coffee in his kitchen next morning. Absolutely confident of all that. Whereas for Adamsberg, the more certain other people's expectations were of him, the more oppressed he felt. It gave him an irresistible urge to disappoint them, to let them down. And then again, he had been thinking a bit too much about his *petite chérie* lately, and would go on doing so, on the slightest pretext. Especially since he had realised during his walk that afternoon that it was nine years now, not eight, since he had last seen her. Nine years, good God! And all at once it had seemed to him that this wasn't normal. He had felt alarmed.

Until now, he had always imagined her travelling the world, in a yacht with some flying Dutchman perhaps, or riding a Berber camel, learning to throw a spear under the guidance of an African tribesman, eating croissants in the Café des Sports et des Artistes in Belleville, or chasing cockroaches in a hotel bedroom in Cairo.

But today he had imagined her dead.

Adamsberg had been so shaken that he had stopped for a cup of coffee, his forehead burning, sweat running down his temples. He visualised her lying dead, having died some time ago, her body decomposing under a tombstone, and in the grave alongside her the little bundle of bones belonging to Richard III. He had tried to summon up images of the Berber camel-handler, the Dutch yachtsman and the café owner in Belleville. He had begged them all to help him reanimate her as usual in front of his eyes, to work the strings and make that tombstone vanish. But damn them all, these characters wouldn't let themselves be summoned up. Leaving the way clear for this deathly fear to grip him. Dead, dead, dead, Camille dead. Yes, surely dead. And he had been imagining her alive all this time, even if she had been unfaithful to him with other men, just as he had been unfaithful to her with other women, even if she had expelled him from her thoughts, even if she was stroking the shoulders of the bellhop in the bed in the Cairo hotel, after he had come to her room to get rid of the cockroaches, even if she was taking photographs of all the clouds in Canada – because Camille collected clouds that looked like people's profiles, which were not easy to come by – and even if she had forgotten Adamsberg's face and his name, just so long as Camille was alive somewhere in this world. Because if so, everything was all right. But if Camille had died somewhere or other in this world, then everything was not all right at all. In that case, what point would there be any more in getting up in the morning and busying oneself, if she were dead, Camille, the unlikely offspring of a Greek god and an Egyptian prostitute (for that was how he saw her origins)? What would be the point after that of bothering to track down murderers, or counting the spoonfuls of sugar in his coffee, or going to bed with Christiane, or looking at the stones in every street, if Camille wasn't somewhere on the planet, making life vibrate around her with her combination of seriousness and frivolity, the seriousness reflected on her forehead, the frivolity on her lips which met together in a perfect figure of eight, an image of the infinite? And if Camille was dead, Adamsberg would have lost the only woman who had said to him quietly one morning: 'Jean-Baptiste, I'm going to Wahiguya. It's on the upper reaches of the Volta.' She had disentangled herself from his arms, had said 'I love you,' dressed, and left. He had thought she was going out to buy bread. But she had not come back, his *petite chérie*. Nine years. He wouldn't have been entirely misleading anyone if he had said to them 'Yes, I know Wahiguya, I even lived there for a while.'

And on top of everything, here was Christiane, quite certain that she would be making the coffee for him in the morning. While the *petite chérie* had died somewhere without his being able to do anything about it. And now, one day, he would die himself, without ever seeing her again. He imagined that Mathilde Forestier might be able to pull him out of this black depression, even if that wasn't the reason he was trying to find her. But he did hope that when he saw her the film would start again, from the right moment, with the bellhop in the Cairo hotel.

Mathilde did telephone.

He told Christiane, who had quickly been disillusioned, to have an early night, since he would be late back; half an hour later, he was talking to Mathilde Forestier.

She welcomed him with a friendliness that loosened the stranglehold the world had exerted on him for the past few hours. She even gave him a kiss, not quite on the cheek and not quite on the lips. She laughed, and said yes she liked doing that, she knew exactly where to plant a kiss, she had an excellent eye for that kind of thing, but he was not to be alarmed, since she never took men her own age as lovers, it was an absolute principle, avoiding comparisons and complications. Then she took his shoulder and led him over to a table, where an old lady was playing patience and sorting the mail at the same time, and where a very tall blind man seemed to be advising her on both counts. The table was oval, and transparent, and had water and fish inside it.

'It's an aquarium-table,' Matilde explained. 'I designed it myself one evening. It's a bit showy, a bit obvious, like me. The fish don't like Clémence playing patience. Every time she slaps a card down on the glass, they shoot off in all directions – look.'

'No good!' sighed Clémence, gathering up the cards. 'It's a

sign. I shouldn't send a reply to the well-preserved M., 66. But he was so tempting. His ad in the paper was so good.'

'Have you replied to many?' asked Charles.

'Two thousand, three hundred and fifty-four. But it's never any good. It's fate. I end up telling myself, Clémence, it's just *not* going to work out.'

'Yes, it will,' said Mathilde, to encourage her, 'especially if Charles helps you write the replies. He's a man, he'll know what appeals to them.'

'The product doesn't seem all that easy to market, though,' observed Charles.

'But I'm *counting* on you to help me find a way,' said Clémence, who didn't seem to take offence whatever anyone said to her.

Mathilde took Adamsberg into her study. 'We'll sit at my cosmic table, if you don't mind. I find it relaxing.'

Adamsberg examined the large table made of black glass and pierced with hundreds of luminous dots lit from below, representing all the constellations in the night sky. It was beautiful, excessively so.

'My tables don't seem to tempt anyone to market them,' Mathilde commented. 'Facing you,' she went on, pointing with her finger at the surface, 'you have Scorpio, the Serpent Holder, the Lyre, Hercules and the Corona Borealis. Do you like it? I like to sit here with my elbows on the south end of Pisces. And the thing is, the whole picture's false. Because the thousands of stars we see shining have already burnt themselves out, so the sky's out of date. You realise what that means, Adamsberg? The sky's out of date. But does that matter, if we can still see it?'

'Madame Forestier,' said Adamsberg, 'I'd like you to take

me to see the chalk circle man tonight. Have you listened to the radio today?'

'No,' said Mathilde.

'This morning we found a woman with her throat cut, inside one of his circles, just a couple of streets away from here, in the rue Pierre-et-Marie-Curie. A nice, ordinary, middle-aged lady, with no secret vices to explain why someone would want to kill her. The chalk circle man has moved up a gear.'

Mathilde lowered her darkened face onto her clenched fists, then stood up abruptly and fetched a bottle of Scotch and two glasses, putting them between the two of them, over Aquila, the Eagle.

'I'm not feeling too good this evening,' Adamsberg said. 'Death is stalking around in my head.'

'I can see that. Have a drink,' said Mathilde. 'Tell me about the woman who had her throat cut. We can talk about the other death afterwards.'

'What other death?'

'There must be another one,' Mathilde said. 'If you get this upset every time you come across a murder, you'd have left the police long ago. So there must be some other death that's tormenting you. Do you want me to take you to the chalk circle man, so you can arrest him?'

'It's too soon. I just want to locate him, see him, find out about him.'

'I feel awkward, Adamsberg. Because this man and I, we've sort of become accomplices. There's a bit more between us than I told you the other day. In fact I've seen him about a dozen times, and from the third time on he realised that I'd spotted him. He keeps his distance, but he still lets me trail him, he glances at me, maybe even smiles, I'm not sure, he's always been too far away to see, and he keeps his head down. But the last time, he even gave a little wave of his hand before he left, I'm convinced. I didn't want to tell you all this the other day, because I didn't want you to put me down as crazy. After all, the police pigeonhole us all, don't they? But now it's different, if the police want him for murder. Adamsberg, this man looks totally inoffensive to me. I've walked along streets at night enough times to be able to scent danger. But with him, no, nothing. He's quite small, very short for a man, slight, neatly dressed, his features are vague, they change, they're hard to remember, but he's not good-looking. I'd put him at about sixty-five. Before he crouches down to write on the pavement he flicks up the tails of his raincoat, so as not to get them dirty.'

'How does he draw the circles – from the inside or the outside?'

'From the outside. He'll stop suddenly, in front of something on the ground, get out his chalk as if he knew right away that this was tonight's object. He looks round, waits till the coast is clear, he certainly doesn't want to be seen, except by me, and he seems to allow that, I don't know why. Perhaps he thinks I understand him. His whole operation takes about half a minute. He draws a big circle round the object, then he crouches down to write his words, still looking round. Then he disappears at the speed of light. He's as quick as a fox and he seems to know his way around. He always manages to lose me once he's drawn the circle, and I've never managed to track him to his home. But anyway, if you arrest this guy, I think you'd be making a big mistake.'

'I don't know,' said Adamsberg. 'I need to see him first. How did you find him in the first place?'

'It wasn't rocket science. I phoned a few journalists I know who'd taken an interest in the case from the start. They gave me the names of the people who'd first reported the circles. I telephoned the witnesses. It may seem odd to you that I got involved in something that's none of my business, but that's because you don't work with fish. When you spend hours of your life studying fish, you start thinking there's something wrong with you, and perhaps it's that you ought to spend less time on fish and more on your fellow human beings, and watch their habits as well. I'll explain that another time. Anyway, practically all these witnesses had discovered the circles before about half past midnight, never any later. And since the chalk circle man seemed to roam all over Paris, I thought, well, he must be taking the metro, and he doesn't want to miss the last connection, so that's a hypothesis to test. Stupid really, isn't it? But two circles had been found only at two in the morning, in the same area, in the rue Notre-Dame-de-Lorette and the rue de la Tour-d'Auvergne. Since they're fairly busy streets, I thought these circles must have been drawn late at night, after the last metro. Perhaps because by then he was going home on foot, because he lived nearby. Is this getting too involved?'

Adamsberg shook his head slowly. He was full of admiration.

'So then I thought, with a bit of luck his nearest metro station must be either Pigalle or Saint-Georges. I lay in wait four nights running at Pigalle: nothing. And yet there were two more circles on those nights in the 17th and 2nd *arrondissements*, but I saw nobody who fitted the bill coming in or out of the metro station between ten and when it closed. So I tried Saint-Georges. And there I noticed a small man on his own, hands stuffed in his pockets, looking at the ground, who took a train at quarter to eleven. I saw a few other people too, who might have been likely suspects. But just this one little man came back out of the metro at quarter past midnight. And four days later he did the same thing. The next Monday, the beginning of a section number one, you'll remember, so a new age, I went back to Saint-Georges. He turned up and I followed him. That was the time with the biro. Because it was him all right, Adamsberg. Other times I would wait at the metro to try and follow him home. But at that point he always manages to give me the slip. I wasn't going to run after him – I'm not the police.'

'I won't tell you that's *fantastic* work, it sounds too much like police talk, but all the same, it is fantastic work.'

Adamsberg often used the word 'fantastic'.

'True,' said Mathilde. 'I did well there, better than with Charles Reyer, at any rate.'

'You *like* him – Reyer?'

'He's a bad-tempered so-and-so, but that doesn't bother me. He makes up for Clémence, the old woman you saw, who's mind-numbingly good-natured. She seems to do it on purpose. Charles won't get a rise out of her any more than with me. That'll teach him, it'll blunt his teeth.'

'*Her* teeth are a bit funny, Clémence's.'

'You noticed, yes, like *Crocidura russula* – more like animal's teeth, aren't they? It must put off the lonely-hearts men she tries to date. We ought to give Charles an eye makeover and Clémence a teeth makeover – we ought to give the world a makeover, really. Then of course it would be perfectly boring. If we get a move on, we could be at Saint-Georges metro station by ten, if that's what you want. But I've already told you, Adamsberg, I really don't think it's him you should be chasing. I think someone else used his circle afterwards. Is that impossible?'

'It would have to be someone who was remarkably familiar with his routine.'

'Like me.'

'Yes, and don't say so too loudly or you'll be suspected of following your chalk circle man that night and then dragging your victim, whom you'd previously knocked out, of course, over to the rue Pierre-et-Marie-Curie, before cutting her throat, on the spot, right in the middle of the circle, making sure she wasn't outside the line. But that seems pretty far-fetched, doesn't it?'

'No. I think that would be quite possible if you wanted to incriminate somebody else. In fact, it's very tempting, this madman who's been offering himself on a plate to the police and drawing his blue chalk circles two metres wide, just big enough to contain a corpse. It could have given plenty of people the idea of committing murder, if you ask me.'

'But how could any prosecutor prove a motive, if the victim turns out to be entirely unknown to the circle man?'

'The prosecutor would think it was a motiveless crime by a lunatic.'

'He doesn't look like a lunatic at all, from all the classic signs. So how could the "real" murderer, according to you, be certain that the circle man would be found guilty in his place?'

'Well, what do you think, Adamsberg?'

'I don't think anything yet, Madame, to tell you the truth. But I've just had a bad feeling about these circles from the beginning. I don't know, just now, whether the man who draws them killed this woman. You could be perfectly right. Perhaps the chalk circle man is just a victim himself. You seem to be much better at working things out and reaching conclusions than I am, you're a scientist. I don't use the same methods, I don't do deductive reasoning. But the feeling I've got at the moment, very strongly, is that this circle man isn't nice at all – even if he is your protégé.'

'But you haven't got any evidence?'

'No. But I've been trying to find out everything about him for weeks. He was already dangerous, in my view, when he was just drawing rings round cotton buds and hairpins. So he's still dangerous now.'

'But good heavens, Adamsberg, you're working backwards! It's as if you were to say that some food was toxic because you felt sick before eating it!'

'Yes, I know.'

Adamsberg seemed irritated with himself: his eyes were heading for dreams and nightmares where Mathilde couldn't follow him.

'Come on, then,' she said, 'let's go to Saint-Georges. If we get lucky and see him, you'll find out why I'm defending him against you.'

'And why's that?' asked Adamsberg, standing up, with a sad smile on his face. 'Because a man who gives you a little wave of his hand can't be all bad?'

He looked at her, his head on one side, his lips curled into a lopsided grin, and he looked so charming that Mathilde felt once more that with this man life was a little better. Charles needed new eyes, Clémence needed a new set of teeth, but this policeman needed a total face makeover. Because his face was crooked, or too small, or too big, or something. But Mathilde would not have let anyone touch it for the world.

'Adamsberg,' she said, 'you're just too cute. You've no business being a policeman, you should have been a streetwalker.'

'Well, I am a streetwalker as well, Madame Forestier. Like you.'

'That must be why I like you so much. But that won't stop me proving to you that my intuition about the chalk circle man is as good as yours. And watch it, Adamsberg, you're not going to lay a finger on him tonight, not in my company. Give me your word.'

'I promise. I won't lay a finger on anyone at all,' said Adamsberg.

At the same time, he was thinking that he would try to keep his word on this in relation to Christiane, who was lying waiting for him, naked, in bed, back at his flat. And yet who would turn down an offer from a naked girl? As Clémence would say, perhaps the evening was jinxed. Clémence seemed to be a bit jinxed herself, in fact. As for Charles Reyer, it was worse than a jinx: he was teetering on the edge of an internal explosion, a major cataclysm.

When Adamsberg followed Mathilde back into the big room with the aquarium, Charles was still talking to Clémence, who was listening attentively and amiably, puffing at a cigarette as if she was new to smoking. Charles was saying:

'My grandmother died one night, because she had eaten too many spice cakes. But the real sensation was next day, when they found my father at the table eating the rest of the cakes.'

'Very interesting,' said Clémence, 'but now I'd like you to help me write my letter to my M., 66.'

'Night-night, children,' said Mathilde on the way out.

She was already in action, striding towards the stairs, in a hurry to be off to the Saint-Georges station. But Adamsberg had never been able to hurry.

'Saint George,' Mathilde called to him, as they scanned the street for a taxi. 'Isn't he the one who killed the dragon?'

'I wouldn't know,' said Adamsberg.

The taxi dropped them at the Saint-Georges metro station at five past ten.

'It's OK,' said Mathilde. 'We're still in time.'

By half past eleven, the chalk circle man had still not shown up. There was a pile of cigarette ends around their feet.

'Bad sign,' said Mathilde. 'He won't come now.'

'Perhaps his suspicions have been aroused,' said Adamsberg.

'Suspicions? What about? That he'd be accused of murder? Rubbish! We don't know if he even listens to the radio. He might not even know about the murder. You already know he doesn't go out every night, it's as simple as that.'

'It's true, he might not have heard the news yet. Or else perhaps he did hear it, and it made him wary. Since he knows someone's watching him, he may be changing his haunts. In fact, I'm sure he will. It's going to be the devil's own job to find him.'

'Because he's the murderer – is that what you mean, Adamsberg?'

'I don't know.'

'How many times a day do you say "I don't know", or "Maybe"?'

'I don't know.'

'I know about all your famous cases so far, and how

successful you are. But all the same, when you're here in the flesh, one wonders. Are you sure you're suited to the police?'

'Certain. And anyway, I do other things in life.'

'Such as?'

'Such as drawing.'

'Drawing what?'

'The leaves on the trees and more leaves on the trees.'

'Is that interesting? Sounds pretty boring to me.'

'You're interested in fish, aren't you?'

'What do you all have against fish? And anyway, why don't you draw people's faces? Wouldn't it be more fun?'

'Later. Later or maybe never. You have to start with leaves. Any Chinese sage will tell you.'

'Later? But you're already forty-five, aren't you?'

'Yes, but I can't believe that.'

'Ah, that's like me.'

And since Mathilde had a hip flask of cognac in her pocket, and since it was getting seriously cold, and since she said, 'We're into a section two of the week now, we're allowed to have a drink,' they did.

When the metal gates of the metro station closed, the chalk circle man had still not appeared. But Adamsberg had had time to tell Mathilde about the *petite chérie* and how she must have died somewhere out in the world, and how he hadn't been able to do anything about it. Mathilde appeared to find this story fascinating. She said that it was a shame to let the *petite chérie* die like that, and that she knew the world like the back of her hand, so she'd be able to find out whether the *petite chérie* had been buried, with her monkey, or not. Adamsberg felt completely drunk because he didn't usually touch spirits. He couldn't even pronounce 'Wahiguya' properly.

At about the same time, Danglard was in an almost identical condition. The four twins had wanted him to drink a large glass of water – 'to dilute the alcohol,' the children said. As well as the four twins, he had a little boy of five, just now fast asleep in his lap, a child whom he had never dared mention to Adamsberg. This last one was the unmistakable offspring of his wife and her blue-eyed lover. She had left this child with Danglard one fine day, saying that all in all it was better that the kids should stay together. Two sets of twins, plus a singleton who was always curled up in his lap, made five, and Danglard was afraid that confessing to all this would make him look a fool.

'Oh, stop going on about diluting the alcohol,' said Danglard. 'And as for you,' he said, addressing the first-born of the older set of twins, 'I don't like this way you've got of pouring white wine into plastic cups, and then pretending that you're being sympathetic, or that it looks nice, or that you don't object to white wine so long as it's in a plastic cup. What's the house going to look like with plastic cups every-where? Did you think of that, Édouard?'

'That's not the reason,' the boy replied. 'It's because of the taste. And then, you know, the flakiness afterwards.'

'I don't want to know,' said Danglard. 'And if we're talking about flakiness, you can take a view on that when the vicomte de Chateaubriand, the greatest writer in French literature, and about ninety-nine beautiful girls, have all rejected *you*, and when you've turned into a Paris cop who may be a sharp dresser but is all mixed up inside. I don't

think you'll ever manage that. What about a case conference tonight?'

When Danglard and his kids had a case conference, it meant
they got to talk about his police work. It could last hours,
and the kids adored it.

'Well, for a start,' said Danglard, 'and can you beat this? St
John the Baptist walked out and left us to deal with this sham-
bles for the rest of the day. That got me so worked up that
by three o'clock I was well away. And yes, it's clear that the
man who wrote that stuff on the other circles *is* the same one
who wrote the stuff round the circle with the murdered
woman in it.'

'Victor, woe's in store, what are you out here for?' chanted
Édouard. 'Or you might as well say "Marcel, go to hell, on
your bike and ring the bell" or "Maurice, call the police, give
us all a bit of peace" or—'

'OK, OK, said Danglard, 'but yes, "Victor, woe's in store"
does suggest something vicious: death, bad luck, a threat of
some kind. Needless to say, Adamsberg was the first to get a
sniff of that. But is that enough for us to charge this man?
The handwriting expert's quite positive about it: the man's
not mad, he's not even disturbed, this is an educated person,
careful about his appearance and his career, but discontented
and aggressive as well as deceptive – those were his words. He
also said, "This man's getting on in years, he's going through
some crisis, but he's in control; he's a pessimist, obsessed about
the end of his life, therefore about his afterlife. Either he's a
failure on the brink of success, or a successful man on the
brink of failure." That's the way he is, kids, our graphologist.
He turns words inside out like the fingers of a glove, he sends
them one way, then the other. For instance, he can't talk about

the desire for hope without mentioning the hope for desire, and so on. It sounds intelligent the first time you hear it, but after that you realise there's nothing there really. Except that it *is* the same man who's been doing all the circles so far, a man who's clever and perfectly lucid, and that he's either about to succeed in life or to fail. But as for whether the dead woman was put into a circle that had already been drawn or not, the lab people say it's impossible to tell. Maybe yes, maybe no. Does that sound like forensic science to you? And the corpse hasn't been much help, either: this is the corpse of a woman who led a totally uneventful existence, nothing odd at all, no complicated love life, no skeletons in the family cupboard, no problems with money, no secret vices. Nothing. Just balls of wool and more balls of wool, holidays in the Loire Valley, calf-length skirts, sensible shoes, a little diary that she wrote notes in, half a dozen packets of currant biscuits in her kitchen cupboard. In fact she wrote about that in her diary: "Can't eat biscuits in the shop, if you drop crumbs the boss notices." And so on and so forth. So you might say, well, what on earth was she doing out late at night? And the answer is she was coming back home after seeing her cousin, who works in the ticket office at the Luxembourg metro station. The victim often used to go over there and sit alongside her in the booth, eating crisps, and knitting Inca-style gloves to sell in the wool shop. And then she would go back home, on foot, probably along the rue Pierre-et-Marie Curie.'

'Is the cousin her only family?'

'Yes, and she'll inherit the estate. But since it consists of the currant biscuits plus a tea caddy with a few banknotes in, I can't see the cousin or her husband cutting Madeleine Châtelain's throat for that.'

'But if someone wanted to use a chalk circle, how would they have known where there was going to be one that night?'

'That is indeed the question, my little ones. But we ought to be able to work it out.'

Danglard got up carefully, to put Number Five, René, to bed.

'For instance,' he resumed, 'take the *commissaire*'s new friend, Mathilde Forestier: it seems that she's actually seen the chalk circle man. Adamsberg told me. Look, I'm managing to say his name again. Obviously the conference is doing me good.'

'At the moment, I'd say it was a one-man conference,' Édouard observed.

'And this woman, who knows the chalk circle man, she worries me,' Danglard added.

'You said the other day,' said the first-born girl of the second set of twins, 'that she was beautiful and tragic and spoilt and hoarse-voiced, like some exotic Egyptian queen, but she didn't worry you then.'

'You didn't think before you spoke, little girl. The other day, nobody had been killed. But now, I can just see her coming into the police station, on some damfool pretext, making a big fuss, getting to see Adamsberg. And then talking to him about this, that and the other, before getting round to telling him she knows this chalk circle man pretty well. Ten days before the murder – bit of a coincidence isn't it?'

'You mean she'd planned to kill Madeleine, and she came to see Adamsberg so that she'd be in the clear?' asked Lisa. 'Like that woman who killed her grandfather but came to see you a month before, to tell you she had a "presentiment"? Remember?'

'You remember that dreadful woman? Not an Egyptian princess at all, and as slimy as a reptile. She nearly got away with it. It's the classic trick of the murderer who telephones to say they've found a body, only more elaborate. So, well, yes. Mathilde Forestier turning up like that does make you think. I can just imagine what she'd say : "But *commissaire*, I'd hardly have come and told you I knew all about the chalk circle man if I was intending to use him to cover up a murder!" It's a dangerous game, but it's bold, and it could be just her style. Because she *is* a bold woman, you've probably gathered that.'

'So did she have a motive for killing poor fat Madeleine?'

'No,' said Arlette. 'This lady, Madeleine, must just have been unlucky, picked by chance to start a series, so they'd pin it on the circle maniac. The real murder'll happen later. That's what papa is thinking.'

'Yes, maybe that is what he's thinking,' Danglard conceded.

VIII

NEXT MORNING, MATHILDE CAME ACROSS CHARLES REYER AT THE foot of the stairs, fumbling with his door. In fact she wondered whether he hadn't been waiting for her, and pretending not to find the keyhole. But he said nothing as she went past.

'Charles,' said Mathilde, 'you're putting your eye to keyholes now, are you?'

Charles straightened up, and his face looked sinister in the dark stairwell.

'That's you, is it, Queen Mathilde, making cruel jokes?'

'Yes, it's me, Charles. I'm getting my retaliation in first. You know what they say: "If you want peace, prepare for war."'

Charles sighed.

'Very well, Mathilde. In that case, please help a poor blind man put the key in the lock. I'm not used to this yet.'

'Here you are,' said Mathilde, guiding his hand. 'Now it's locked. Charles, what did you think of that cop who came round last night?'

'Nothing. I couldn't hear what you were saying, and anyway I was distracting Clémence. What I like about Clémence is that she's got a screw loose. Just to know there are people like that in the world does me good.'

'Today my plan's to follow someone else like that, a man who's interested in the mythical rotation of sunflower stems, goodness knows why. It could take me all day and the evening as well. So if it's not too much trouble, I'd like you to go and see the policeman for me. It's on your way.'

'What are you up to, Mathilde? You've already got what you were after, whatever that was, by getting me to come and live here. You want me to get my eyes sorted out, you get me to babysit Clémence for a whole evening, and now you're flinging me into the arms of this policeman. Why did you come looking for me? What are you trying to do with me?'

Mathilde shrugged.

'You're making too much of it, Charles. We met in a cafe, that's all. Unless it's to do with underwater biology, my impulses generally don't have any particular reason. And listening to you, I'm sorry I don't have more of a reason for them. Then I wouldn't be standing here, stuck on the stairs, having my morning spoiled by a blind man with a bad temper.'

'I'm sorry, Mathilde. What do you want me to say to Adamsberg?'

Charles called his office to tell them he would be late. First, he wanted to run the errand for Queen Mathilde and go to the police station; he wanted to help her out, to do something to please her. And this evening he would like to be friendly, to admit that he had placed his hopes in her, and tell her, perfectly courteously, that he had carried out the errand perfectly courteously. He didn't want to murder Mathilde, that was the last thing in the world he wanted. For now, he wanted to cling on to Mathilde, doing his best not to let go of her, not to spin round and slap her in the face. He wanted to go on listening to her talking, about anything and everything, with her husky voice and her tightrope-walking ways, always on the brink of missing her step. Perhaps he should bring her some jewellery this evening, a gold brooch? No, not a gold brooch, a cooked chicken with tarragon, she would surely prefer some chicken with tarragon. And then he could listen to the sound of her voice, and drop off to sleep with warm champagne in his pyjama pockets, if he had had pyjamas. Or pockets. Certainly not tear her eyes out, not massacre her, absolutely not, no, he would buy her a cooked chicken. With tarragon.

He should have arrived at the police station by now, but he wasn't sure. It wasn't one of the buildings whose location he had managed to map in his head. He would have to ask. Hesitating, he scraped the pavement ahead of him with his stick, walking slowly. He was lost in this street, obviously. Why had Mathilde sent him here? He began to feel desperately tired. And when he felt that way, anger was sure to follow, welling up in lethal pulses from his stomach into his throat, until it invaded his whole head.

Danglard, feeling seedy and with a blinding headache himself, was just arriving for work. He saw the very tall blind man standing stock-still near the door of the station, an expression of arrogant despair on his face.

'Can I help you?' Danglard asked. 'Are you lost?'

'Are *you*?' Charles asked.

Danglard ran his hand through his hair.

What a mean question. Was he lost?

'No,' he said.

'Wrong,' said Charles.

'Is that any of your business?' said Danglard.

'Is my standing here any of your business?'

'Oh, for crying out loud,' said Danglard. 'Suit yourself. Stay lost if you're lost.'

'I'm looking for the police station.'

'Well, you're in luck, I work there. I'll take you in. What do you want the police station for?'

'It's about the chalk circle man,' Charles said. 'I've come to see Jean-Baptiste Adamsberg. He's your boss, isn't he.'

'That's right,' said Danglard. 'But I don't know if he's here yet. He could still be wandering around somewhere. Are you coming to tell him something, or to ask him for something? Because I have to tell you that the boss doesn't give out precise information, whether you ask him for it or not. So if you're a journalist, you'd do better to go and join your colleagues over there. There are plenty of them about.'

They were arriving at the entrance to the station. Charles stumbled against the step and Danglard had to catch him by the arm. Behind his glasses, in his dead eyes, Charles felt a brief spasm of rage.

He said quickly: 'No, I'm not a journalist.'

Danglard frowned and rubbed a finger over his forehead, although he knew perfectly well that you couldn't cure a hangover by rubbing your head.

Adamsberg was there. Danglard could not have said afterwards whether he was in the office or even sitting down. He had perched there, too light for the big armchair and too dense for the white and green furnishings.

'Monsieur Reyer wants a word with you,' said Danglard.

Adamsberg looked up. He was more struck than he had

been the previous day by Charles's face. Mathilde was right: the blind man was spectacularly good-looking. And Adamsberg admired beauty in others, although he had given up wishing for it himself. In any case, he couldn't remember ever having wanted to be anyone else.

'You stay too, Danglard,' he said. 'Haven't seen you for some time.'

Charles felt around for a chair and sat down.

'Mathilde Forestier can't come to the Saint-Georges metro station with you tonight as she had promised. That's the message. I'm just dropping in to deliver it to you.'

'How am I supposed to find him without her, this circle man, since she's the only one who knows who he is?' asked Adamsberg.

'She thought of that,' said Charles, with a smile. 'She said I could do it, because she thinks the man leaves a vague smell of apples behind him. She says all I have to do is wait with my nose in the air and breathe deeply, and I'd be pretty good at sniffing out the smell of rotten apples.'

Charles shrugged.

'It wouldn't work, of course. She can be very perverse.'

Adamsberg looked preoccupied. He had swivelled sideways, putting his feet on top of the plastic waste bin, and was resting a piece of paper on his thigh. He seemed to want to start drawing as if he was entirely unconcerned, but Danglard thought this was far from the case. He could see that Adamsberg's face was darker than usual: the nose seemed sharper and he was clenching and unclenching his jaw.

'Yes, Danglard,' he said rather quietly. 'We can't do anything if Madame Forestier isn't there to guide the way. Odd, don't you think?'

Charles made as if to leave.

'No, Monsieur Reyer, don't go,' said Adamsberg, still in a quiet voice. 'An annoying thing happened – I had an anonymous phone call this morning. A voice that said: "Did you see an article two months ago in the local newsletter, *The Fifth Arrondissement in Five Pages*? Why don't you question the people who actually *know* something, *commissaire*?" Then they hung up. Here's the paper, I had someone find it for me. Just the local rag, but a lot of people get to see it. Here, Danglard, can you read this bit out, top of page two. You know I'm no good at reading out loud.'

A well-informed lady?

If certain gentlemen of the press can't resist recording the antics of some poor devil who gets his kicks drawing chalk circles round bottle tops, like a five-year-old, that is, alas, a sign of the weird idea our colleagues have of their calling. But when serious scientists poke their noses in, it hardly bodes well for French research. First we had the eminent psychiatrist, Vercors-Laury, writing a column about this sad individual. But he's not alone. Gossip in the quartier *suggests that Mathilde Forestier, the world-famous underwater specialist, has also decided to start analysing this pathetic exhibitionist. She has apparently made it her business to get to know him, and even to accompany him on his grotesque nocturnal perambulations. That would make her the only person who has penetrated the 'mystery of the chalk circles'. A brilliant achievement, wouldn't you say? She apparently revealed as much, one evening in the* Dodin Bouffant, *at the launch of her latest book, when*

94

serious quantities of alcohol were consumed. Naturally,
our *arrondissement has prided itself on having the cele-*
brated Madame Forestier as one of our long-standing
residents, but would she not do better to spend her govern-
ment grant on chasing her beloved fish instead of running
after an imbecile who may be a criminal, or a deranged
lunatic, a man whom her childish imprudence might even
attract to our district, which has so far been spared any
circles? Some fish are deadly poisonous, even on the
slightest contact. Madame Forestier knows this perfectly
well: far be it from us to teach her to suck eggs. But what
does she know about the poisonous fish that might roam
at large in the city streets? By encouraging this kind of
behaviour, is she not stirring up trouble in the depths of
society? Why is she trying to hook this creature and drag
him into our arrondissement, *something that must distress*
all law-abiding inhabitants?

'So,' said Danglard, putting the newspaper down on the
desk, 'the person who called you must have heard about the
murder yesterday, or this morning, and contacted you right
away. Someone with prompt reactions who doesn't like
Madame Forestier, it would seem.'

'What do you conclude, then?' asked Adamsberg, still sitting
sideways and grinding his jaw.

'I conclude that, thanks to this article, quite a few people
have known for some time that Madame Forestier was in
possession of certain little secrets. They might want to get
their hands on that knowledge themselves.'

'Why would they want to do that?'

'Optimistic hypothesis: to provide copy for the newspapers.

Pessimistic hypothesis: to bump off their mother-in-law, stick her inside a chalk circle and make everyone think it was the work of the latest maniac in Paris. The idea could have crossed the minds of a few benighted individuals too cowardly to risk an attack in the open. It offered them a golden opportunity, and all they had to do was find out the habits of the chalk circle man. After a few drinks, Mathilde Forestier would be an ideal source of information.'

'And then what?'

'Then one might tend to ask, for instance, how it happened that Monsieur Charles Reyer went to live in Mathilde's house a few days before the murder.'

Danglard was like that. He didn't mind coming out with remarks of this kind, in front of the people he was accusing. Adamsberg couldn't bring himself to be so direct, and he found it useful that Danglard had no qualms about hurting people's feelings. Qualms that made Adamsberg say anything except what he was really thinking. Which in police matters produced unexpected, and not always immediately helpful, results.

After Danglard's words there was a long silence. Danglard was still pressing his finger to his forehead.

Charles had suspected that there might be a trap, but all the same he couldn't help giving a start. In the dark inside his head, he imagined Adamsberg and Danglard both looking at him.

'Very well,' said Charles, after a pause. 'I did start renting from Mathilde Forestier last week. Now you know as much as I do. I have no wish to answer your questions or to defend myself. I don't understand anything about this beastly business of yours.'

'Nor do I,' said Adamsberg.

Danglard was annoyed. He would have preferred Adamsberg not to admit his ignorance in front of Reyer. The *commissaire* had started scribbling on the paper resting on his knee. It was provoking to see Adamsberg taking that casual, vague and passive attitude, not asking any questions to move the situation on.

'All the same,' Danglard insisted, 'why did you want to rent her apartment?'

'Bloody hell!' said Charles, exploding with anger. 'It was Mathilde who came to find me in my hotel to offer me the flat, not the other way round.'

'But you chose to go and sit by her in the café, before that, didn't you? And you told her, for some reason, that you were looking for a place to rent.'

'If you were blind, you'd know it's beyond my powers to recognise someone sitting on a café terrace.'

'I think you're capable of doing plenty that's so-called beyond your powers.'

'That'll do,' said Adamsberg. 'Where is Mathilde Forestier now?'

'She's off tracking some guy with a bee in his bonnet about the rotation of sunflowers.'

'Since we can't do anything and we don't know anything,' Adamsberg said, 'let's drop it.'

This argument appalled Danglard. He suggested that they search for Mathilde, in order to find out more straight away. They could post a man outside her house to wait for her, or send someone to the Oceanographical Institute.

'No, Danglard, we're not going to bother with that. She'll be back. What we *will* do, though, is post some men tonight at the metro stations of Saint-Georges, Pigalle and Notre-Dame-de Lorette, with a description of the chalk circle man. That will keep our consciences clear. And then we'll wait. The man who smells of rotten apples will start his night-time walks again – it's inevitable. So we'll wait. But we haven't any hope of catching him. He's bound to alter his itinerary.'

'But what's the point of our worrying about the circles if he isn't the killer?' said Danglard, getting up and pacing awkwardly round the room. 'The chalk circle man! Again! But surely we don't give a damn about the poor sod! It's whoever's using him that we're after!'

'Not me,' said Adamsberg. 'So we carry on looking for the circle man.'

Danglard stood up again, wearily. It would take time to get accustomed to Adamsberg.

Charles could sense all the confusion in the room. He perceived Danglard's vague discomfiture and Adamsberg's indecision.

'Which one of us is going into this blind, you or me, *commissaire*?' asked Charles.

Adamsberg smiled.

'I don't know,' he said.

'After the anonymous phone call, I suppose you'll be wanting me to "help you with your inquiries",' Charles went on.

'I don't know about that,' said Adamsberg. 'But anyway there's nothing to stop you going to work as usual. Don't worry.'

'It's not my work that worries me, *commissaire*.'

'I know. It was just an expression.'

Charles heard the sound of pencil on paper. He imagined that the *commissaire* must be drawing while he was talking.

'I don't know how a blind man could manage to kill someone. But I'm a suspect now, aren't I?'

Adamsberg made an evasive gesture.

'Let's say you picked the wrong moment to go and live at Mathilde Forestier's house. Let's say that, for whatever reason, we've recently become interested in her and what she knows, that is if she's told us everything, which may not be the case. Danglard can explain all that to you. Danglard's incredibly intelligent, you'll see. It's a great comfort to work with him. Let's also say that you seem to be a rather awkward customer, which doesn't help.'

'What makes you think that?' asked Charles, with a smile – a nasty smile, Adamsberg thought.

'Madame Forestier says so.'

For the first time, Charles felt worried.

'Yes, that's what she says,' Adamsberg repeated. '"He's a bad-tempered so-and-so, but that doesn't bother me" is what she said. And you like her too. Because being in touch with Mathilde, Monsieur Reyer, would do you a power of good, it would bring back shining black eyes, like patent leather. She'd do plenty of people good. Danglard doesn't like her, though – no, Danglard, you don't. He's taken against her, for reasons that he'll tell you about. He's even tempted to cast doubts on her good faith. He's already finding it odd that our Mathilde turned up at the police station to talk to me about the chalk circle man with or without a smell of apples, long before the murder. And he's quite right. It *is* odd. But then, everything's odd about this case. Even the rotten apples. Anyway, the only thing we can do now is wait.'

Adamsberg started doodling again.

'All right,' said Danglard. 'We'll wait.'

He was not in a good mood. He saw Charles to the street.

Returning to the corridor, he was still pressing a finger to his forehead. Yes, it was true: because he had this long body in the shape of a skittle he resented Mathilde, who was the kind of woman who'd never go to bed with someone whose body was that shape. So, yes, he would have liked her to be guilty of something. And this business with the newspaper article certainly landed her in it. That would interest the kids, for sure. But he had sworn, since his mistake about the girl in the jeweller's shop, never to proceed unless he had evidence and hard facts, not some half-baked hunch that wormed its way into your head. So he would have to tread carefully with Mathilde.

Charles remained on edge all morning. His fingers trembled a little as they ran over the Braille perforations.

Mathilde was on edge too. She had just lost sight of the sunflower man. Stupid, really – he had jumped into a taxi. She had found herself standing on the Place de l'Opéra, disappointed and disoriented. If it had been in the first half of the week, she would have sat down immediately and ordered a glass of beer. But since it was the second half, there was no point getting too upset. Should she pick someone at random to follow? Why not? On the other hand, it was almost midday and she wasn't far from Charles's office. She could call and take him out to lunch. She had been a bit brusque with him that morning, with the excuse that during a section two you could say what you liked, and she felt rather bad about that now.

She caught Charles by the shoulder just as he came out of the building in the rue Saint-Marc.

'I'm hungry,' said Mathilde.

'Good thing you found me,' said Charles. 'All the cops in the world are thinking about you now. You were the subject of a minor denunciation this morning.'

Mathilde had settled herself on a banquette at the back of the restaurant, and nothing in her voice indicated to Charles that this item of news disturbed her.

'All the same,' Charles insisted, 'it wouldn't take much for the police to start thinking you're the person best placed to help the murderer. You're probably the only one who could have told him the time and place to find a circle that would suit his plan to kill someone. Worse still, you could even become a murder suspect yourself. With your bad habits, Mathilde, you're going to be in deep trouble.'

Mathilde laughed. She ordered several dishes. She really was hungry.

'Well, that's just fine,' said Mathilde. 'Strange things happen to me all the time. It's my fate. So one more or less isn't going to make any difference. The night of the *Dodin Bouffant* was surely in a section two of the week, and I must have had too much to drink and talked a lot of nonsense. I don't remember a lot about that evening, to be honest. You'll see – Adamsberg will understand, he won't go chasing the impossible all over the world.'

'I think you're underestimating him, Mathilde.'

'I don't think I am.'

'Yes, you are. Plenty of people underestimate him, though probably not Danglard, and certainly not me. I know, Mathilde, Adamsberg has this voice that lulls you to sleep, it charms you and makes you drop your guard, but he never relaxes at all. His voice has distant pictures and vague thoughts in it, but it's leading inexorably to some conclusion, although he may be the last to suspect that himself.'

'Have you finished? Is it all right if I eat my lunch?'

'Of course. But listen to what I'm saying: Adamsberg doesn't attack, but he transforms you, he weaves his way round you, he comes at you from behind, he leads you on, and in the end he disarms you. He can't be caught out and tracked down, not even by you, Queen Mathilde. He'll always get away, because of his gentleness and his sudden indifference. So to you or me or anyone else, he can be a good thing or a bad thing, like the sun in spring. It all depends how you expose yourself to it. And for a murderer he'd be a formidable enemy – you ought to realise that. If I'd killed someone I'd prefer to have a cop chasing me whose reactions I could predict, not one who's as hard to grasp as water, then suddenly turns to stone. He flows like a stream, he resists like a rock, he's on his way to his destination, the estuary. And a murderer could easily drown in that.'

'A destination? An estuary? Don't be silly, that's ridiculous,' said Mathilde.

'Maybe his destination is the lever that lifts up the whole blasted world. Or the blasted eye of the blasted cyclone – another eye for you, Mathilde. Or some outpost of the universe where knowledge exists, in the mists of eternity. Ever thought of that, Mathilde?'

Mathilde had stopped eating.

'You really impress me, Charles. You come out with all this stuff like a book, but you just listened to him for an hour this morning.'

'I've developed the sense instincts of a dog,' said Charles

bitterly. 'A dog that hears what people don't hear, and smells what they can't smell. Some wretched hound that will travel a thousand kilometres as the crow flies, just to get back home. So I go about things a different way from Adamsberg, but I've got some knowledge too. That's all we have in common. I believe I'm the most intelligent person on the planet, and my voice is like a metal-cutter. It slices things up, it twists them and my brain operates like a machine, sorting out data. And for me there are no destinations or estuaries any more. I don't have the strength or purity now even to imagine that cyclones have eyes. I've given up all that, I'm too tempted by the nasty little tricks and ways I can find every day to compensate for what I can't do. But Adamsberg doesn't need any distractions in order to stay alive, do you understand what I'm saying? He just gets on with his life, letting it all swill about, big ideas and little details, impressions and realities, thoughts and words. He combines the belief of a child with the philosophy of an old man. But he's real and he's dangerous.'

'You *do* impress me,' repeated Mathilde. 'I can't say I've dreamed of having a son like you, because he would have driven me up the wall, but you impress me. I'm starting to see why you don't give a damn about fish.'

'You're probably the one who's right, Mathilde, because you find something to love in slimy creatures with round eyes that aren't even good to eat. But it wouldn't bother *me* if all the fish in the sea were dead.'

'You certainly have the gift of giving me impossible ideas for a section two of the week. You've even upset yourself – look, you're sweating. Don't get so steamed up about Adamsberg. He's a nice guy, isn't he?'

'Oh yes,' said Charles. 'He's a nice guy all right. He says nice things, does Adamsberg. And I can't understand why that doesn't worry you.'

'You do impress me, Charles,' Mathilde repeated.

IX

STRAIGHT AFTER LUNCH, ADAMSBERG DECIDED TO TRY SOMETHING.
Inspired by the little diary they had found on the dead woman, he bought a small notebook that he could slip into his back pocket. So that if he was struck by some interesting thought he could write it down. Not that he was hoping for any miracles. But he told himself that when the notebook was full, the overall effect might be relevant and perhaps provide him with some insight into himself.

He felt that he had never been living so much from day to day as at this moment. He had already noted on many occasions that the more pressing anxieties he had, harassing him with their urgency and seriousness, the more his brain seemed to want to play dead. In response, he did his best to live by concentrating on little things, as if he were some stranger who cared about nothing, wiping out any thoughts and qualities, keeping his spirit a blank, his heart empty and his mind fixed entirely on short wavelengths. This state, a stretch of indifference which discouraged all those around him, was well-known to him now, but he found it hard to control. Because when he was in this uncaring mode, having rid himself of all the worries of the planet, he felt calm and on the whole happy. But as the days went by, such indifference insidiously caused internal damage so that everything became colourless. People began to become transparent to him, all identical, since they were so distant from him. And this lasted until, coming to some end point in his informal disgust with the world, he felt that he himself had no density, no importance at all, letting himself be ferried along by other people's daily lives, being all the readier to carry out a host of little kindnesses since he had become completely detached from them. His body's mechanisms and his automatic responses enabled him to get through the day, but he wasn't there for anyone. At this stage, almost out of his own existence, Adamsberg felt no anxiety, had no thoughts. This disinterest for the world did not even have the panic-inducing fear of nothingness. His spiritual apathy did not bring with it the dread of ennui.

But God in heaven, it had happened very quickly this time.

He could perfectly well remember the extreme distress which only yesterday had struck him when he had imagined that Camille was dead. And now even the word 'distress' seemed meaningless to him. What could distress mean? That Camille was dead? But what did that matter now? Madeleine Châtelain had had her throat cut, the chalk circle man was still on the loose, Christiane was pusuing him, Danglard was depressed, and he had to deal with the whole bloody mess, but what was the point?

So he sat down in a café, took out his notepad and waited. He surveyed his thoughts as they proceeded through his head. They seemed to have a middle, but no beginning and no end. So how could he write them down? Disgusted but still calm, after an hour he wrote:

'Can't think of anything to think'.

Then from the café he telephoned Mathilde. Clémence Valmont answered the phone. The old woman's grating voice brought him a sense of reality, the idea of doing something before he completely lost touch with things and passed out. Mathilde had returned home. He wanted to see her, but not at her house. He gave her an appointment for five o'clock at his office.

Unexpectedly, Mathilde arrived on time. She had surprised even herself.

'I don't understand,' she said. 'It must be the effect of "helping the police with their inquiries".'

Then she looked at Adamsberg, who was not drawing but was sitting with his legs outstretched, one hand in his trouser pocket, the other holding a cigarette in his fingertips and seeming so disorganised and nonchalant that it was hard to know how to approach him. But Mathilde sensed that he was quite capable of doing his job, even looking like that, or perhaps especially when looking like that.

'I get the feeling this isn't going to be as much fun as last time,' said Mathilde.

'You could be right,' said Adamsberg.

'It's ridiculous going to all this performance of getting me called to the station. You would have done better to come to the Flying Gurnard, and we could have had a drink and a bite to eat. Clémence has made a repulsive sort of dish, her local speciality, she says.'

'Where's she from?'

'Neuilly.'

'The Paris suburbs aren't exactly exotic. But I'm not staging any kind of performance. I just needed to talk to you and I didn't want to sit cosily in the Flying Gurnard or anywhere else you might have in mind.'

'Because a policeman doesn't eat dinner with his suspects?'

'On the contrary, that's just what he does do,' said Adamsberg wearily. 'Being on matey terms with the suspects is precisely what the books recommend. But over in your house, it's like a railway station. Blind men, batty old women, students, philosophers, upstairs neighbours, downstairs neighours – you have to be one of the Queen's courtiers or you're nothing at all, isn't that right? And I don't like the choice of courtier or nothing. But I don't know why I'm bothering to say all this, it's not important.'

Mathilde laughed.

'I get it,' she said. 'In future we should meet in a café or on a bridge over the Seine, some neutral territory where we'd be on equal terms. Like two republican French citizens. Mind if I smoke?'

'Go ahead. That article in the 5th *arrondissement* newsletter, Madame Forestier, did you know about it?'

'Never heard of the damn thing till Charles recited it from memory for me at lunch time today. And as for whatever I was shouting about at the *Dodin Bouffant*, it's no good trying to get me to remember it. All I can tell you is that when I've had a few drinks, my stories multiply reality by about thirty. It's not impossible that I boasted that the chalk circle man came to dinner with me, and shared my bath, or my bed, or that we planned his nocturnal tricks together. Once I start showing off, nothing is too outrageous. So, you can imagine. Sometimes I act like a natural disaster, as my philosopher friend takes care to tell me.'

Adamsberg pulled a face.

'I find it hard to forget you're a scientist,' he said. 'I don't think you're as unpredictable as you make out.'

'So, Adamsberg, you think I cut Madeleine Châtelain's throat? It's true I don't have a respectable alibi for that evening – nobody checks when I come and go. There's no man sharing my bed at the moment, and there's no concierge for our block: I'm as free as the wind, as free as the mice. So what is this poor woman supposed to have done to me to prompt this?'

'Everyone has their secrets. Danglard would say that since you spend your time following thousands of people, Madeleine Châtelain could figure somewhere in your notes.'

'It's not impossible.'

'He would add that in your underwater career you are known to have slit the bellies of two blue sharks. You're capable of determination, courage and strength.'

'Oh, come on, you're not going to shelter behind someone else's arguments, are you? Danglard this, Danglard that. What about you?'

'Danglard's a thinker. I listen to what he says. In my view, only one thing matters: the chalk circle man and his wretched outings. Nothing else. Take Charles Reyer, now – what do you know about him? It's impossible to tell which of you first sought the other out. It looks as if it was you, but perhaps he forced your hand.'

There was a silence, then Mathilde said:

'Do you really think I'd allow myself to be manipulated like that?'

At this difference in her tone, Adamsberg interrupted the doodling he had started. Sitting opposite, she was staring at him, smiling, grand and generous, very sure of herself, regal, as if she could demolish his office and the rest of the world with a simple mocking remark. So he spoke slowly, chancing some new ideas suggested by her expression. Resting his cheek on his hand, he said:

'When you came to the police station the first time it wasn't because you were looking for Charles Reyer, was it?'

Mathilde laughed.

'Yes, I was looking for him! But I could have found him without your help, you know.'

'Of course. It was stupid of me. But you're a splendid liar. So what game are we playing here? Who were you really looking for? Me?'

'Yes, you.'

'Simple curiosity, because my appointment had been announced in the papers? You wanted to add me to your collection? No, it wasn't that.'

'No, of course not,' said Mathilde.

'To talk about the chalk circle man, as Danglard thinks?'

'No, not even that. If it hadn't been for the press cuttings you had under the desk lamp, I wouldn't have thought of that. You're free not to believe me, of course, now that you know I'm thoroughly unreliable.'

Adamsberg shook his head. He felt he was on the wrong track.

'It was because I got a letter,' Mathilde continued. 'It said: "I have just heard that Jean-Baptiste has been appointed to a job in Paris. Please go and take a look." So I came to take a look, as was natural. There are no coincidences in this life, as you well know.'

Mathilde inhaled smoke, with a smile. She was really enjoying all this, was Mathilde. Yes, she was having a ball, in her damned section of the damned week.

'Tell me the rest, Madame Forestier. Who was the letter from? Who are we talking about?'

'Our beautiful traveller. Sweeter than me, more shy, less disreputable, less bohemian. My daughter Camille, my daughter. But you were right in one respect, Adamsberg. Richard III is dead.'

Afterwards, Adamsberg could not have said whether Mathilde left immediately or a little while later. Disconnected as he was at this moment, one thing had echoed round inside in his head. She was alive, Camille was alive. His *petite chérie*, never mind where, never mind who she was with, she was breathing, her obstinate forehead, her tender lips, her wisdom, her futility, her silhouette, they were all alive and well.

Only later, as he was walking home – having posted men for the night at the Saint-Georges and Pigalle metro stations, despite a feeling that it was pointless – did he realise what he had learned. Camille was Mathilde Forestier's daughter. Well, of course. Even though Mathilde was a great mystifier, there was no point bothering to check it out. Profiles like that weren't mass-produced.

There is no such thing as coincidence. His *petite chérie*, somewhere in the world, had read a French newspaper and learned about his posting, then had written to her mother. Perhaps she wrote to her often. Perhaps they even saw each other often. It was possible indeed that Mathilde managed to make the destinations of her scientific expeditions corres-pond to wherever her daughter was at the time. In fact, Adamsberg was certain of it. He would only have to find out which coasts Mathilde had been working from for the last few years to know where Camille had been. So he had been right. She had been travelling, lost and out of reach.

Out of reach. He realised that. He never would manage to catch hold of her. But she *had* wanted to know what was happening to him. He hadn't melted from her mind like wax. But then he had never had any doubt about that. Not that he thought himself unforgettable. All the same, he felt that a little piece of him had lodged like a tiny stone, somewhere in Camille, and that she too must be carrying him round inside her like a weight, infinitesimal though it might be. It was inevitable. It had to be. However vain human love appeared to him, and however dark his feeling today, he could not admit that some magnetised fragment of that love was not still lodged somewhere in Camille's body. Just as he knew, although he rarely thought about it, that he had never allowed Camille's existence to dissolve from inside himself, though he couldn't have said why, because he had not consciously thought about it.

What bothered him, and even distracted him from the far country where his mood of indifference had taken him, was that now he would only have to ask Mathilde to find out. Just to find out. To find out, for instance, whether Camille loved someone else. But it was better not to know, and to keep on imagining the bellhop in the Cairo hotel where he had left off last time. The bellhop was good-looking, dark, with long eyelashes, and it was just for a couple of nights, since he had got rid of the cockroaches in the bathroom. And in any case, Mathilde wouldn't tell him. They wouldn't speak about it any more. Not a word about the girl who was taking both of them on journeys from Egypt to the Paris suburbs, and that was that. But what if she really was in the Paris suburbs? She was alive, that was all that Mathilde had wanted to tell him. So she had kept the promise she had made the other night at the Saint-Georges metro station. She had removed that death from his head.

Perhaps too, since Mathilde felt herself under threat from the police and their harassing questions, she had been setting out to make herself untouchable. To let him know that if he went on harassing the mother he would distress the daughter. No, that wasn't Mathilde's style. There was no future in talking about it any more; it was a closed subject, full stop. He had to leave Camille wherever she was, and carry on the inquiries surrounding Madame Forestier without deviating from his course. That was what the investigating magistrate had said earlier that afternoon. 'No deviating from the course of the inquiry, Adamsberg.' But what course? A course assumed a plan, some future laid out ahead, and in this case Adamsberg had less of a plan than ever before. He was waiting for the chalk circle man. This man didn't seem to trouble many people. But for him, the man behind the circles was a creature who laughed at night and pulled cruel faces during the day. A man who was difficult to catch, disguised, putrid and feathery like moths of the night, and the thought of him was repulsive, giving Adamsberg the shivers. How could Mathilde possibly think the man was 'harmless' and take a ridiculous pleasure in following him around as he drew his deadly circles? That was an example, whatever he might say, of Mathilde's fantastic recklessness. And how could Danglard, the learned and deep Danglard, also be certain this man was innocent, expelling him from his thoughts, whereas in Adamsberg's mind he was crouching like a malevolent spider? But perhaps he, Adamsberg, was going desperately wrong? Too bad, if so. He had only ever been able to follow his own train of thought, wherever it took him. And whatever happened, he would keep on chasing this deadly man. And he *would* see him, he had to. Perhaps when he saw him he would change his mind. Perhaps. He would wait. He was sure that the chalk circle man would come to him. The day after tomorrow. The day after tomorrow, perhaps, there would be a new circle.

He had to wait another two days, long enough to make one think that the circle man was obeying some kind of rule and didn't operate at weekends. Not until the Monday night did his quarry pick up the chalk again.

A patrolling officer discovered a blue chalk circle in the rue de La Croix-Nivert at six in the morning.

This time, Adamsberg accompanied Danglard and Conti.

The object on the ground was a plastic model of a swimmer, about the size of his thumb. This effigy of a baby, lost in the middle of a huge circle, produced a certain malaise. That's deliberate, thought Adamsberg. Danglard must have thought the same thing at the same moment.

'This lunatic's winding us up,' he said. 'Putting a human figure in the circle after the murder the other day . . . He must have searched for ages to find this doll, or else he brought it along with him. Though that would be cheating.'

'He's no lunatic,' Adamsberg said. 'It's just that his pride is getting piqued. So he's starting to make conversation.'

'Conversation?'

'Well, communicating with us, if you like. He held out for several days after the murder, longer than I thought he would. He's changed his haunts and he's more elusive now. But he's starting to talk. He's saying: "I know there's been a murder, but I'm not scared of anything, and to prove it, here we go again." And it'll carry on. No reason he should stop talking now. He's on a slippery slope. The slope of language. Where he's no longer sufficient unto himself.'

'There's something unusual about this circle,' Danglard observed. 'It's not drawn the same way as the others. It's the same writing, that's for sure. But he's gone about it differently, wouldn't you say, Conti?'

Conti nodded.

'The other times,' said Danglard, 'he drew the circle in one go, as if he was walking round and drawing at the same time, without stopping. Last night he drew two semicircles meeting up, as if he did one side first and then the other. Has he lost the knack in five days?'

'Yes, that's true,' said Adamsberg, with a smile. 'He's getting careless. Vercors-Laury would find that interesting – and he'd be right.'

Next morning, Adamsberg called the office as soon as he was up. The man had been drawing circles again in the 5th *arrondissement*, in the rue Saint-Jacques, just a stone's throw from the rue Pierre-et-Marie-Curie where Madeleine Châtelain had been killed.

Carrying on the conversation, thought Adamsberg. Something along the lines of 'Nothing's going to stop me drawing my circle near the murder scene.' And if he didn't actually draw it in the rue Pierre-et-Marie-Curie itself, it was simply out of consideration, a matter of taste if you like. This man is refined.

'What's inside the circle?' he asked.

'Some tangled cassette tape.'

While listening to Margellon's report, Adamsberg was leafing through the mail from his letter box. He had in front of him a letter from Christiane, passionate in tone, repetitive in content. Leaving you. Egotistical. Don't want to see you again. Have my pride. And so on for six pages.

All right, we'll think about that tonight, he told himself, feeling sure that he was indeed egotistical, but having learned from experience that when people are really leaving you they don't bother to warn you with six-page letters. They just go without a word, like the *petite chérie*. And people who walk about with the handle of a revolver sticking out of their pockets never kill themselves either, as some poet whose name he couldn't remember had said, in more or less those words. So Christiane would probably be back, with plenty of demands. Complications ahead. Under the shower, Adamsberg resolved not to be too mean, and to think about her tonight, if he could remember to think about her.

He arranged to meet Danglard and Conti in the rue Saint-Jacques. The tangled cassette tape lay like spilled intestines in the morning sun, in the centre of the big circle, drawn with a single line this time. Danglard, a tall weary figure, his fair hair thrown back, was watching him approach. For some reason, perhaps because of his colleague's apparent fatigue, or his air of being a defeated thinker who was still persevering in his enquiries into destiny, or because of the way he folded and unfolded his large, dissatisfied and resigned body, Adamsberg found Danglard touching that morning. He felt the urge to tell him again that he really liked him. At certain moments, Adamsberg had the unusual gift of making short sentimental declarations which embarrassed other people by their simplicity, of a kind not habitual between adults. He quite often told a colleague he was good-looking, even when it wasn't true, and whatever the state of indifference he was undergoing at the time.

For the moment, Danglard, in his impeccable jacket, but preoccupied by some secret worry, was leaning against a car. He was jingling coins in his trouser pocket. He's got money worries, Adamsberg thought. Danglard had owned up to having four children, but Adamsberg already knew from office gossip that he had five, that they all lived in three rooms with this providential father's salary as their only income. But nobody felt pity for Danglard, nor did Adamsberg. It was unthinkable to feel pity for someone like him. Because his obvious intelligence generated a special zone around him, about two metres in radius, and you took care to think before speaking when you entered the zone. Danglard was more the object of discreet watchfulness than of gestures of help. Adamsberg wondered whether the 'philosopher friend' mentioned by Mathilde generated a zone like that, and how broad it was. The said philosopher friend seemed to know quite a bit about Mathilde. Perhaps he had been at the evening event at the *Dodin Bouffant*. Finding out his name and address and going to see him and question him would be a minor police task, to be carried out without broadcasting it. Not the sort of thing that tempted Adamsberg as a rule, but this time he thought he would take it on himself.

'There's a witness,' said Danglard. 'He was already at the station when I left. He's waiting there for me now to make his statement.'

'What did he see?'

'At about ten to midnight a small thin man passed him, running. It was only when he heard the radio this morning that he made the connection. He described an elderly man, slight build, thinning hair, in a hurry and carrying a bag under his arm.'

'That's all?'

'He left behind him, it seemed to this witness, a slight smell of vinegar.'

'Vinegar? Not rotten apples?'

'No. Vinegar.'

Danglard was in a better mood now.

'A thousand witnesses, a thousand noses,' he added, smiling and spreading wide his long arms. 'A thousand noses, a thousand different interpretations. A thousand interpretations probably add up to a thousand childhood memories. One person thinks of rotten apples, another vinegar, and tomorrow we might have people talking about what? Nutmeg, furniture polish, strawberries, talcum powder, dusty curtains, cough mixture, gherkins . . . The circle man must have a smell that reminds people of their childhood.'

'Or the smell of a cupboard,' said Adamsberg.

'Why a cupboard?'

'I don't know. But childhood smells come from cupboards, don't they? All sorts of smells get mixed up together, it makes a sort of universal smell.'

'We're getting off the point,' said Danglard.

'Not that much.'

Danglard realised that Adamsberg was starting to float again, to disengage, or whatever he did; at any rate the already vague connections in his logic were being relaxed, so he proposed they should go back to the station.

'I'm not coming with you, Danglard. Take the statement from the vinegar witness without me – I feel like hearing what Mathilde Forestier's "philosopher friend" has to say.'

'I thought you weren't interested in Madame Forestier's case.'

'No, correction, she does *interest* me, Danglard. I agree with you. She's blocking our path here. But she doesn't seriously bother me.'

In any case, thought Danglard, so few things did seriously bother his *commissaire* that he wasn't going to hang about thinking of them. Wait a minute, though. Yes, the story of the stupid dog that drooled and all the rest of it, that had seriously bothered him, and still did. And there were other things of the same order, as he would one day discover, perhaps. It was true, this irritated him. And the better he got to know Adamsberg, the more mysterious his boss became, as unpredictable as a night creature whose heavy, bumbling but effective flight wears out anyone trying to catch it. But he would have liked to borrow some of Adamsberg's vagueness and uncertainty, the times when his gaze seemed to be dying or burning by turns, making you want either to get away from him or to get closer to him. He thought that if he had Adamsberg's gaze, he might see things start to wobble, to lose their clear reasonable contours, like trees shimmering in a summer heat haze. Then the world would seem less implacable to him, he would stop wanting to understand every tiny little detail about everything, exploring the remotest areas of the heavens. He would feel less exhausted as a result. But as it was, only white wine enabled him to take his distance, for a brief and, as he knew, artificial moment.

X

As Adamsberg had been hoping, Mathilde was not at home. He found her elderly assistant, Clémence, leaning over a table covered with photographic slides. On a chair alongside her lay a newspaper, open at the personal ads.

Clémence was too chatty to be intimidated by him. She wore several layers of nylon overalls, one on top of the other, like onion skins. A black beret was perched on her head, and she was smoking a military-strength Gauloise. She hardly opened her mouth when she spoke, so it was hard to get a glimpse of the famous pointed teeth for which Mathilde liked to provide zoological comparisons. She wasn't timid, she wasn't vulnerable, she wasn't bossy, yet her manner wasn't exactly affable either. Clémence was such an odd individual that one couldn't help wanting to listen to her for a while, to find out what it was, underneath all the banal trappings behind which she barricaded herself, that fuelled her energy.

'How were the small ads today?' Adamsberg asked.

Clémence shook her head doubtfully.

'Not up to much, monsieur. See this one: "Male, retired, fond of quiet life, own maisonette, seeks female companion, under 55, with taste for eighteenth-century engravings." Engravings? Not my cup of tea. Or this one: "Pensioner, ex-retail trade, seeks attractive woman, nature lover, for friendship, more if we click." Nature lover? No, I don't think so. They all write the same thing, never the truth. What they really should say is: "Self-centred old creep, running to seed, seeks young woman for sex." Why don't people say what they mean? Makes you waste a lot of time. Yesterday, now, I tried three of these, *none* of them any good. What it is, though, the minute they see what I look like they lose interest. So it's pointless, really. But, my sakes, what else can I *do*, I ask you?'

'You're asking *me*? But why are you so keen to find a husband, Clémence?'

'That's a question I don't ask, monsieur. You're probably thinking, poor old Clémence, she's a bit funny in the head because her fiancé disappeared long ago, leaving her a note. Ah, but you'd be wrong, because I didn't care then, when I was twenty, and I don't care now. Tell you the truth, monsieur, I'm not so keen on men. No, it must be for a bit of excitement in life. Can't think of anything else to do, that's the long and short of it. Plenty of women are like that, you want my opinion. I'm not so keen on women either, tell you the truth. They all think, like me, you get married, that's it, it'll give you a purpose in life. And you know what, I go to church as well. But if I didn't keep doing all this, what would I do? I'd probably be out shoplifting, pinching things, spitting at people in the street. Well, there we are, Mathilde thinks I've got saving graces. *Better* to be nice in this world, isn't it? Less trouble.'

'What about Mathilde?'

'If it wasn't for Mathilde, monsieur, I'd still be waiting for a miracle down at the metro station. It's *lovely* being here with her. I'd do anything to help Mathilde.'

Adamsberg didn't try to disentangle all the contradictory messages he was getting. Mathilde had told him that Clémence could call something blue for an hour and red for the next hour, and made up stories about her life depending on who she was talking to. You would need to listen to Clémence for months before you could work out what it all meant. You'd need to be determined. Or a psychiatrist, some would say. But even that would be too late. Everything seemed to be too late for Clémence, that was clear enough, but somehow Adamsberg couldn't feel sorry for her. Maybe Clémence *did* have some saving graces, give her the benefit of the doubt, but she wasn't very appealing, so he wondered why Mathilde had felt like giving her lodgings in the first place, up there in the Stickleback, and then hiring her as an assistant. Now if there was a *good* person in the basic sense of the word, it was Mathilde. Haughty and sarcastic, but courteous and consumed with generosity. It struck you with violence in Mathilde, and more tenderly in Camille. Danglard, however, didn't agree about Mathilde.

'Does Mathilde have any children?'

'A daughter, monsieur. *Very* beautiful. Would you like to see a photo?'

Suddenly Clémence had become genteel and respectful. It was perhaps time to take what he had come for, before her mood changed again.

'No, no photos, please,' said Adamsberg. 'What about her friend, the philosopher, do you know him?'

'You're asking a lot of questions, monsieur. This isn't getting Mathilde into trouble, is it?'

'Not at all – on the contrary, so long as we can keep this confidential.'

This was the kind of police trick that Adamsberg disliked, but how else was he to answer questions like that? So he brought out his formulae like his multiplication tables, to move things on.

'I've seen him twice,' said Clémence with a touch of pride, dragging on her cigarette. 'He wrote this.'

She spat out a few shreds of tobacco, reached over to the bookshelf and held out a thick book towards Adamsberg. *The Subjective Zones of Consciousness* by Réal Louvenel. Réal, that was a French-Canadian name. Adamsberg allowed a few recollections evoked by the name to swim up in his memory. None of them was very distinct.

'He used to be a doctor,' Clémence was saying in her distinctive closed-mouth way of speaking. 'Supposed to be a great genius, I warn you. I don't know if you'd be able to keep up with his talk. Not wanting to give offence, but you've got to be on the right wavelength to understand a *word* he says. Mathilde seems to know what he's on about. What I can tell you is that he lives on his own with twelve Labradors. Imagine! Phew, his place must stink!'

Clémence had switched out of genteel mode. It hadn't lasted. Now she was being the village idiot again. Then, suddenly, she came out with:

'And what about you, anyway? This circle man, is that interesting? What do you want out of life? Are you in a mess, like everyone else?'

The old woman was going to unsettle Adamsberg soon, something that happened only rarely. Not that her questions embarrassed him. They were perfectly ordinary questions. He just found that everything about her made him uncomfortable: her clothes, her pinched lips, her hands in gloves so as not to smudge the slides, her weird bursts of conversation. If Mathilde was kind enough to rescue Clémence from her troubles, that was fine. But he didn't want to be involved. He had the information he had come for, that would do. He withdrew, muttering a few polite words so as not to hurt her feelings.

Taking his time, Adamsberg looked up the address and phone number of Réal Louvenel. A male voice, strident and highly strung, replied that he could see him that afternoon.

Réal Louvenel's house did indeed stink of dog. He was a man constantly in motion, so completely unable to sit for long in a chair that Adamsberg wondered how he managed to write anything at all. He found out afterwards that the philosopher dictated his books. Although he replied quite willingly to Adamsberg's questions, Louvenel was doing half a dozen other things at the same time: emptying an ashtray, putting papers in the bin, blowing his nose, whistling to one of the dogs, strumming on the piano, doing up his belt another notch, sitting down, getting up again, closing the window, stroking the arm of his chair. A fly wouldn't have been able to keep up with him, still less Adamsberg.

Adapting as best he could to this exhausting nervous energy, Adamsberg tried to register the information that emerged from Louvenel's complex sentences, making strenuous efforts not to let himself be distracted by the sight of the philosopher as he ricocheted off all the surfaces of the room, or by the hundreds of photographs pinned to the walls, mostly representing litters of Labradors, or youths in a state of undress. He understood Louvenel to say that Mathilde would have been more eminent and a deeper thinker if she didn't always allow her instincts to distract her from her original projects, and that they had known each other since their university days, when they'd sat together at lectures. Then he said that during the evening at the *Dodin Bouffant* she'd had a bit too much to drink, and had caused a sensation among the customers by saying that she and the chalk circle man were big pals, that only she and he understood anything about the 'metaphorical renaissance of the pavement as a new field of scientific endeavour'. She had also announced that the wine was excellent and that she would like another glass, that she had dedicated her latest book to the chalk circle man, that his identity was no mystery to her, but that this man's painful existence would remain a secret, a 'Mathildism'. As it might be an 'esoterism'. A 'Mathildism' was something she would tell nobody else about, though in any case it was of no intrinsic interest.

'Since I couldn't stop the flow, I left without hearing the end,' Louvenel concluded. 'I find Mathilde embarrassing when she's had a few drinks. She gets boring, talkative, trying as hard as she can to get everyone to love her. Don't *ever* let her start drinking when you're with her.'

'Did anyone else in the café seem particularly interested in what she was saying?'

'I seem to recall that people were laughing.'

'But why do you think Mathilde follows people in the street?'

'The short answer could be that she collects oddities,' said Louvenel, fiddling with the creases in his trousers and then with his socks. 'You could say that these people she preys

126

on are like her fish, she spots them in the street, she chases after them, then she pigeonholes them. But really it's the opposite. Mathilde's problem is that she'd be perfectly capable of going and living alone under the sea. Yes, she's made it her life's work, she's a tireless researcher and a distinguished scientist, but all that means very little to her. The real draw is the territory she's found for herself, underwater. Mathilde is the only deep-sea specialist I know who won't let anyone accompany her – which is actually very dangerous. "I want to be afraid of everything, and understand everything for myself, Réal, and to go down when I feel like it into a deep trench, into the origins of the Earth." That's how she is. Mathilde is a piece of the universe. Since she can't dissolve into it, she's made up her mind to study it, so as to grasp its hugest physical dimensions. But the ocean takes her away from human society, and she realises that. Because she's also got a big slice of good-heartedness, or generosity if you like, that can't be satisfied with the underwater life. So at regular intervals she comes back to the surface, and gives in to the other temptation, the one that draws her to people, I mean people, not humanity. So she makes her peace with all the millions of little steps people take as they tread the Earth's crust. She takes everything to extremes, and every scrap of behaviour she can capture, wherever it is, seems a miracle to her. She memorises it all, she notes it all, she "Mathildises" it all. And she picks up lovers along the way, because she's quite capable of love. And then when she's tired of all that, when she thinks she has loved her fellow creatures enough, she goes diving again. That's why she follows strangers in the street. To get a kick out of the flicker of someone's eyelids or the twist of an elbow, before she goes off again to defy the immensity of the universe on her own.'

'And what about you? Does the chalk circle man suggest anything to you?'

'Don't think I'm being arrogant, but I'm not interested in such infantile things. Even murder I consider infantile. Child-adults bore me, they're cannibals. They're fit only to feed off other people's vitality. They can't perceive themselves. And because they can't perceive themselves, they can't live unaided, they're greedy for the sight and the blood of other people. Since they have no self-perception, they bore me. You may know that it is man's self-perception that interests me – note that I'm saying perception, sensation, not understanding, or analysis – more than all other human approaches, even if I live from day-to-day expedients like everyone else. That's all I can say about the chalk circle man and his murder, about which I know next to nothing anyway, except that Mathilde talks about him a good deal too much.'

Réal was retying his shoelaces as he spoke.

Adamsberg sensed that Réal Louvenel had made an effort to adapt his way of speaking to his interlocutor. He didn't feel annoyed with him. As it was, he couldn't be sure that he had exactly understood what this excitable man had meant by self-perception, which was clearly a key word for him. But while listening to the philosopher he had started to think about himself, inevitably – as did everyone else, no doubt. And he had felt that while being unable to observe himself, he did indeed 'perceive himself', perhaps in precisely the way Louvenel meant, if only because he sometimes felt 'un-comfortable at being conscious'. He knew that this perception of one's own existence could take underground paths, where one's boots became embedded in mud, and where no answer was forthcoming, and that one needed physical courage not to dismiss it all from one's mind and get rid of it. But he didn't dismiss the feeling when it came over him, since it was a moment when he felt quite sure that to do so would doom him to being nothing at all.

At any rate, the chalk circle man didn't seem to be worrying anyone else. But Adamsberg was untroubled that nobody else was willing to accompany him in his apprehension. That was his own business. He left Louvenel to his fidgety movements, which had calmed down considerably once he had taken a small yellow tablet. Adamsberg deeply distrusted all medicines, and preferred to drag himself round with a high temperature all day rather than take any kind of pill. His little sister had told him that it was very presumptuous always to hope that he would come through it on his own, and that nobody had yet lost their identity by taking an aspirin. His little sister could be a pain sometimes, you wouldn't believe.

Back at the station, Adamsberg found Danglard quite far gone. He had acquired some companions to help him start on the afternoon's bottle of white wine earlier than usual. Sitting round his desk, as if round a café table, Mathilde Forestier and the handsome blind man were knocking the wine back merrily in plastic cups. Things were getting noisy.

Mathilde's resonant voice rang out above the din, and Reyer kept his face turned towards the Queen, looking happy. Adamsberg mentally noted once more the blind man's prodigiously beautiful profile, but it annoyed him to see Reyer keeping his eyes firmly fixed on Mathilde, if that was the right expression. And why in the world should that annoy him?

Was it because he sensed that the blind man was going to be snapped up by Mathilde? No. Mathilde was no ordinary woman, and she would lay no nasty traps in which the weaker party is devoured. But at the same time, when someone laid a hand on Mathilde it was difficult just now not to see a hand being laid on Camille. No, he mustn't confuse them. And anyone had the right to touch Camille, this was a salutary principle he had long ago established. But perhaps it was that Danglard too seemed on the point of being drawn in, despite having been so categorically opposed to Mathilde. It looked as if the two men were engaged in some kind of contest as they sat around the table; the scene smacked of tried and tested seduction gambits, and it had to be admitted that Mathilde, being by now well launched into the white wine, was not insensitive to the atmosphere. After all, she had a perfect right. And Danglard and Reyer too had a perfect right to act like teenagers if they felt like it. What was coming over him, pushing him to act the censor and dictate rules of conduct? Had his own conduct been above reproach toward the young woman in the flat downstairs, with whom he had spent the night? No, not at all. Although a little taken back by the opportunity when it had presented itself, he had chosen his words carefully and had applied his own rules meticulously throughout. But had his conduct towards Christiane been above reproach? Absolutely not; much worse. That reminded him that he hadn't remembered to think about her. So he might as well have a drink with the others. And ask himself what the hell they were doing there anyway.

When he looked more closely, Danglard was not as carried away as all that by the charms of the two suspects sitting at his table. And if one looked more closely again, Danglard the thinker was watching, observing, listening and provoking, however drunk he might appear. Even in his cups, for Danglard's incisive brain Mathilde and Reyer remained a couple of people rather too closely mixed up in a murder case. Adamsberg smiled and went over to the table.

'I know,' said Danglard, indicating the wine, 'it's against the rules. But these persons are not here to see me officially. They're just passing through. It was you they wanted to see.'

'And how!' said Mathilde.

From Mathilde's face, Adamsberg could tell that she was furious with him. Better avoid a row in front of everyone. He gave up on the idea of a drink and took them into his office, making a conciliatory sign to Danglard. But Danglard couldn't have cared less – he had already returned to his paperwork.

'So. It seems that Clémence didn't hold her tongue?' Adamsberg inquired gently of Mathilde as he sat sideways at his desk.

'Why should she?' said Mathilde. 'Apparently you badgered her with a whole lot of questions about her own life and then about Réal. Adamsberg, for heaven's sake, what kind of behaviour is that?'

'Police behaviour, I suppose,' said Adamsberg. 'But I didn't badger her. Clémence has plenty to say for herself unaided, even if she whistles through her teeth. And I wanted to meet Réal Louvenel. I've just got back from seeing him.'

'I know!' said Mathilde. 'And that *really* makes me see red!'

'That's perfectly normal,' said Adamsberg.

'What did you want to see him for?'

'To find out what you said at the *Dodin Bouffant*.'

'For God's sake, what's so important about that?'

'Sometimes, but only sometimes, I'm tempted to find out what people are concealing from me. And according to that article in the 5th *arrondissement* newsletter, you've been acting like a flytrap for anyone who wants to get close to the chalk circle man. So I have to take an interest. I think you have a pretty good idea who he is. I had hoped you would have said a bit more that evening, and that Louvenel would have told me about it.'

'I never imagined you'd go in for such underhand dealings.'

Adamsberg shrugged.

'What about you, Madame Forestier? The first time you came into the police station. Was that straightforward dealing?'

'I had no choice,' said Mathilde. 'But you're supposed to be an honest man. And all of a sudden you've turned slippery.'

'I've got no choice, either. Anyway, that's how I am, I'm slippery. I have to change all the time.'

Adamsberg rested his chin on his hand, still facing sideways. Mathilde was watching him.

'It's as I said,' Mathilde continued. 'You're amoral – you should have been a prostitute.'

'Just what I am being, in order to get information.'

'About what?'

'About him. The chalk circle man.'

'Well, you're going to be disappointed. I made it all up about the identity of the circle man, based on a few vague memories. I've got no proof of any of it. Pure invention.'

'Little by little,' murmured Adamsberg, 'I'm managing to extract a few fragments of the truth. But it takes a long time.

Would you be able to tell me who he is? Even if you're making it up, it still interests me.'

'It's not based on anything serious. Only the circle man reminds me of someone I used to follow some years ago, over by Pigalle too, as it happens. I used to follow this particular man to a dark little restaurant where he lunched alone. He worked while he was eating, and never took his raincoat off. He covered his table with piles of books and papers. And when he dropped something, which happened all the time, he would lift up the hem of his raincoat as if it was a bridal train, whenever he bent down to pick it up. Sometimes his wife would come along, with her lover, to have coffee with him. Then he looked pathetic, desperate to accept any humiliation in order to hang on to whatever was left. But when the wife and her lover had gone, he would be seized with rage, he'd stab at the paper tablecloth with his knife and obviously he was pretty upset. In his place I would have had a drink, but he seemed not to touch alcohol. I noted in my book at the time "Little man greedy for power but doesn't have it. How will he get out of this?" See, I tend to make snap judgements. Réal tells me that too: "Mathilde, you make too many snap judgements." Then I stopped bothering with this man, he made me feel sad and edgy. I follow people to do myself good, not to go poking about in their misery. But when I saw the circle man, and his habit of holding the hem of his coat when he bent down, it reminded me of someone. I looked through my notebooks and remembered the little man who was greedy for power but had none at all, and I thought "Well, why not? Is this perhaps the way he's found to exercise some kind of power?" Another snap judgement, and that's where I left it. You see, Adamsberg, you're disappointed, aren't you?

It wasn't worth making all those underhand visits to my place and Réal's to get this kind of pointless information.'

But Mathilde's anger had subsided.

'Why didn't you tell me all this in the first place?' Adamsberg asked her.

'I wasn't sure about it, I had no evidence. And anyway, you must have noticed that I feel rather protective towards the circle man. Perhaps he has nobody but me on his side. That makes it a duty I can't escape. And anyway, hell's bells, I would hate to think that my personal notes would get into police files as reports on someone.'

'Quite understandable,' said Adamsberg. 'Why did you use the word "greedy" about him? Funny thing, Louvenel used the same word. At any rate, when you were holding forth at the *Dodin Bouffant* you attracted a lot of attention. Anyone would only have had to come to you to find out more.'

'But why?'

'Like I said before. The manic ways of the circle man are an encouragement to murder.'

As he spoke, using the term 'manic' for convenience, Adamsberg remembered that Vercors-Laury had explained to him that the man did not in fact present any of the characteristics of a compulsive mania. And that rather pleased him.

'You didn't get any unusual visits after the night at the *Dodin Bouffant* and the newspaper article?' he went on.

'No,' said Mathilde. 'Unless perhaps all the visits I get are unusual.'

'After that night, did you follow the circle man any more?'

'Yes, of course, several times.'

'And nobody else was around?'

'I didn't notice anything. But I wasn't particularly bothered anyway.'

'What about you?' said Adamsberg, turning towards Charles Reyer. 'What have you come along for?'

'I'm accompanying madame, *monsieur le commissaire.*'

'Why?'

'For something to do.'

'Or to find out more. They tell me that when Mathilde Forestier goes diving, she goes alone, contrary to the rules of the profession. She's not in the habit of taking someone along to accompany or protect her.'

The blind man smiled.

'Madame Forestier was furious. She asked me if I wanted to come and witness the meeting. I said yes. It gives me something to do at the end of the day. But I'm disappointed too. You managed to calm her down rather too quickly.'

'Don't you believe it,' said Adamsberg, with a smile. 'She's got plenty more lies up her sleeve. But did *you*, for instance, know about the article in the 5th *arrondissement* magazine?'

'It's not published in Braille,' said Charles crossly. 'But yes, I heard about it. Happy now? And Mathilde, does that bother you? Does it scare you?'

'Couldn't give a damn either way,' said Mathilde. Charles shrugged and ran his fingers under his dark glasses.

'Someone mentioned it at the hotel,' he went on. 'One of the guests standing in the lobby.'

'See?' said Adamsberg, turning to Mathilde. 'News travels fast, it even reaches people who can't read. And what did he say, this guest in the lobby?'

'Something like "That deep-sea diving lady is at it again.

Now she's pally with the madman who does the circles." That's all I heard. Not very informative.'

'Why did you tell me so willingly that you knew about it? It puts you in an awkward position. You know that you're already regarded with some suspicion. You arrived at Mathilde's by some sort of miracle, and you've got no alibi for the night of the murder.'

'You know that, do you?'

'Naturally – Danglard's been doing his job.'

'If I hadn't told you myself, you would have tried to find out and you would have found out. Better to avoid being detected in a lie, isn't it?'

Reyer gave one of those wicked smiles with which he would have liked to carve up the universe.

'But I *didn't* know,' he added, 'that the person I spoke to in the café in the rue Saint-Jacques was Madame Forestier. I only made the connection later.'

'Yes,' said Adamsberg, 'you already told me that.'

'Well, you repeat yourself too.'

'It's always like that at certain moments in an investigation. People repeat themselves. Then the press reports that "the police are baffled".'

'Sections two and three,' sighed Mathilde.

'And then, suddenly, things move on,' said Adamsberg, 'and you don't have time to say anything.'

'Section one,' added Mathilde.

'You're right, Mathilde,' said Adamsberg, looking at her. 'Same as in everything else. It all goes either too slowly or too fast.'

'Not very original as an idea,' muttered Charles.

'I often say unoriginal things,' said Adamsberg. 'I repeat

myself, I make obvious remarks – in short, I disappoint people. Does that never happen to you, Monsieur Reyer?'

'I try not to let it happen,' said the blind man. 'I detest banal conversations.'

'They don't bother me at all,' said Adamsberg.

'That'll *do*,' said Mathilde. 'I don't like it when the *commissaire* starts talking like this. We'll get nowhere. I prefer to wait for your investigation to make a leap forward, *commissaire*, and then your eyes will light up again.'

'Not a very original idea, either,' said Adamsberg with a smile.

'It's true that in her poetico-sentimental metaphors, Mathilde does not flinch from the grossest banalities,' remarked Reyer. 'Though they're different from yours.'

'Have you two quite finished? Can we just go now?' said Mathilde. 'You're perfectly exasperating, the pair of you. In your different ways.'

Adamsberg waved his hand and smiled, and found himself alone.

Why had Charles Reyer found it necessary to say: 'That's all I heard'?

Because he had heard more than that. Why, then, had he confessed to a fragment of the truth? To stop inquiries going any further.

So Adamsberg called the Hôtel des Grands Hommes. The porter on duty remembered the article in the newsletter and what the guest had said. And yes, of course he remembered the blind man too. How could you forget a blind man like Reyer?

'Did Reyer want to know any more about the article?' asked Adamsberg.

'Yes, indeed, *monsieur le commissaire*,' said the porter. 'He asked me to read the whole thing out to him. Otherwise I might not have remembered.'

'And how did he react?'

'Hard to say, *monsieur le commissaire*. He used to have an icy smile that made you feel like a moron. That day he was smiling like that, but I never knew what that meant.'

Adamsberg thanked him and hung up. Charles Reyer had wanted to find out more. And he had accompanied Mathilde to the station. As for Mathilde, she certainly knew more about the chalk circle man than she was letting on. But of course none of that might be important. Thinking about this kind of information made Adamsberg feel tired. He got rid of it by passing it on to Danglard. If necessary, Danglard would do whatever had to be done better than he would. So now he could go on thinking about the chalk circle man without distraction. Mathilde was right, he was waiting for a sudden leap in the inquiry. And he also knew what she had meant about his eyes lighting up. Cliché though it might be, it means something when you say that a person's eyes light up. It happens or it doesn't. In his case, it depended on the moment. And just now he knew that his gaze was lost far out to sea.

XI

THAT NIGHT ADAMSBERG HAD A DISTURBING DREAM, A combination of pleasure and outlandishness. He saw Camille come into his room, wearing a bellhop's uniform. Looking serious, she undressed and lay down alongside him. Although he realised he was dreaming, and that he was on a slippery slope, he had not resisted. Then the Cairo bellhop had appeared in person and burst out laughing, holding up ten fingers to indicate 'I married her ten times.' Next, Mathilde had arrived, saying, 'He wants to arrest you', and had dragged her daughter away from him. He had clung on to her. He would rather die than lose her to Mathilde. And he had realised that his dream was degenerating, and that the initial pleasure had vanished, so it would be best to put a stop to everything by waking up. It was four in the morning.

Adamsberg got out of bed, cursing.

He paced up and down in his flat. Yes, he was on a slippery slope. If only Mathilde had not told him that Camille was her daughter, she would not have come back into his life with a reality that he had kept at bay for years.

No. That wasn't right. It had started with that sudden

feeling she was dead. That was when Camille had re-emerged from the far-off horizons where he had imagined her, fondly but distantly. But he had already made the acquaintance of Mathilde by then, and her Egyptian profile must have suggested Camille to him more strongly than before. That was how it had begun. Yes, that had been the start of the dangerous series of sensations resounding inside his head, as his memories were being prised up like slates in a high wind, opening gaps in a roof which had previously been carefully maintained. The slippery slope, dammit. Adamsberg had always placed little hope or expectation in love, not that he was opposed to feelings, which would have been pointless, but they weren't the central thing in his life. That was just how it was, a deficiency on his part, he sometimes thought, or an advantage, as he thought at other times. And he never questioned this absence of belief in them. Nor was he about to do so tonight, more than any other night. But as he paced round the flat, he realised that he would have liked to hold Camille in his arms, if only for an hour. Being unable to do so frustrated him; he closed his eyes to imagine it, which didn't help. Where was Camille? Why wasn't she here, to lie in his arms until morning? Realising that he was a prisoner of a desire that could never be fulfilled, not now, not ever, exasperated him. It wasn't so much the desire itself, since Adamsberg never allowed himself to be the prisoner of pride. It was the impression he had of wasting his time and his dreams in a futile and recurrent fantasy, knowing that life would have become much easier long ago if he had been able to forget it. And that was exactly what he had been unable to do. What wretched bad luck it had been to run into Mathilde.

Unable to get back to sleep, he walked through the office

door at five past six in the morning. So he was there to take the call ten minutes later from the police station in the 6th *arrondissement*. A circle had been spotted on the corner of the boulevard Saint-Michel and the long and deserted rue du Val-de-Grace. In its centre lay a pocket English-Spanish dictionary. Feeling out of sorts after his bad night, Adamsberg seized the opportunity to go back into the fresh air. A uniformed policeman was already there, guarding the blue chalk circle as if it were the holy shroud. The man was standing stiffly to attention beside the small dictionary. A ridiculous sight.

'Am I going down some blind alley?' Adamsberg wondered.

Twenty metres further down the boulevard, a café was already open. It was seven o'clock. He sat at an outside table and asked the waiter if the establishment stayed open late, and if so who was on duty between eleven-thirty and half past midnight. He thought that in order to get to the Luxembourg station the chalk circle man would have had to go past this café, that is if he was still using the metro. The proprietor came out to speak to him in person. His attitude was rather aggressive until Adamsberg showed him his card.

'I recognise that name,' the café owner said. 'You're a famous detective.'

Adamsberg let this pass without comment. It made it easier to talk informally.

'Yes,' the café owner said after hearing him out. 'Yes, I did see someone a bit suspicious who could be the one you're after. It would have been just after midnight, he went past here, trotting along rather fast, when I was moving the tables on the terrace and shutting up shop. See these plastic chairs? They're awkward, they fall over, they catch on things. One of them fell on its side, and he tripped up on it. I went over to help him up, but he pushed me away without a word, and off he went fast as he came, with a sort of satchel under his arm, that he kept tight hold of.'

'Sounds like him,' said Adamsberg.

The sun was just reaching the terrace. He stirred his coffee. Things were looking up. Camille was returning to her place in the far distance.

'Did he remind you of anything?' he asked.

'No. Yes . . . I did think, poor old soul, I say that because he was a skimpy little chap. I thought there goes some poor bloke who's been out for a drink, and he's scurrying home, because his wife's going to tear him off a strip.'

'Male solidarity,' Adamsberg muttered to himself, with a sudden feeling of distaste for the man. 'Why did you think he'd been drinking? Because he wasn't too steady on his legs?'

'No, that's not it, because now I think about it he was quite nimble, not clumsy. Perhaps he smelled of drink, though again, I can't say I noticed that at the time. It's just coming back to me, now you mention it. Second nature to me, of course, the smell of drink, my work. You can show me anyone and I can tell you how many he's had. But this little chap the other night, I'd say he'd had a few shorts. Yes, you could smell it all right.'

'What? Whisky? Wine?'

'N-no.' The man hesitated. 'Neither of those. Sweeter than that. Something like those little glasses of liqueur that you see old codgers knocking back over a game of cards. Just a nip at a time, doesn't look much, but it hits the spot in the end.'

'Calvados? Poire?'

'Oh, now you're asking, I'll start making things up if you carry on like that. I didn't have any reason to smell his breath, after all.'

'So maybe it was some fruit liqueur . . . ?'

'Does that tell you anything?'

'Yes, it does, a lot,' said Adamsberg. 'Would you be good enough to go round to the station sometime today, and get someone to take a statement from you? Here's the address. And above all, don't forget to tell my colleague about the fruity smell.'

'I said drink, not fruit.'

'As you like. Doesn't matter.'

Adamsberg smiled, feeling satisfied. He thought once more of his *petite chérie* but now it was as if she were a bird flying past in the distance, nothing more. Relieved, he left the café. Today he would send Danglard round to Mathilde's to try to winkle out of her the address of the restaurant where she had seen the sad man in the raincoat and with papers strewn on the table. You never know.

But he would prefer not to meet Mathilde himself today.

As for the blue circle man, he was still chalking away, not far from the rue Pierre-et-Marie-Curie. Still at it, still holding this one-sided conversation.

And he, Adamsberg, was waiting for him.

XII

DANGLARD HAD MANAGED TO EXTRACT THE ADDRESS OF THE restaurant in Pigalle from Mathilde, but it had closed down two years earlier.

Throughout the day, Danglard kept a watchful eye on Adamsberg's changing moods. Danglard felt that the investigation was dragging. But he recognised that there was not much to be done about it. He had devoted himself to going through Madeleine Châtelain's life with a toothcomb, without finding the least irregularity anywhere. He had also been to see Charles Reyer, to ask him to explain why he had been so curious about the article in the newsletter. Reyer was both taken aback and put out, and above all vexed that his attempt to conceal anything from Adamsberg had been so ineffective. But Reyer was rather taken with Danglard, and the deep and languid tones of this weary man, whom he imagined to be tall, disturbed him less than the too-gentle voice of Adamsberg. His answer to Danglard was simple. As a student of animal anatomy, he had had occasion to attend some of Madame Forestier's seminars in the past. That could be checked out. At the time, he had not had any grudge against anyone, and he had appreciated Madame Forestier for what she was: intelligent and attractive, and he had never forgotten a word of the lectures she had given. Afterwards, he had wanted to wipe this whole period out of his life. But when the client in the hotel foyer had mentioned 'the lady who goes deep-sea diving' the memory of those days had been pleasant rather than otherwise, so he had wondered if the article was about her, and if so what she was being accused of. Reyer gathered that Danglard was prepared to accept this version of events. Danglard nevertheless asked him why he hadn't said all that to Adamsberg the day before, and why he hadn't told Mathilde that he had already realised who she was, on the occasion of their 'chance' meeting in the rue Saint-Jacques. Reyer had replied to the first question that he didn't want Adamsberg to complicate life for him, and to the second that he didn't want Mathilde to think of him as one of those eternal students who as they get older are still acolytes of their professor. Which he had no desire to be.

So all in all, there wasn't much to be gleaned from that, Danglard told himself. Just the usual bundle of half-truths that waste everyone's time. The children would be disappointed. But he felt resentment towards Adamsberg for these dreary days, punctuated only on the mornings when the circles reappeared.

He had the unjustified impression that Adamsberg was exerting a malign influence on the passage of time. The police station itself seemed to be impregnated with the particular behaviour of the *commissaire*. Castreau was no longer fuming over trifles, and Margellon was making fewer stupid remarks – not that the former was becoming milder or the latter more intelligent, rather that it wasn't worth their while to react so strongly all the time. On the whole – but perhaps it was just an impression generated by his own worries – there were fewer outbursts and the usual little rows about nothing were less in evidence, being replaced by a sort of nonchalant fatalism which seemed more dangerous to him. All the officers seemed to be handling the sails of the ship routinely, without showing the least concern if the vessel was momentarily becalmed when the wind dropped. Everyday police matters took their course – three muggings in the street yesterday, for instance. Adamsberg came and went, disappeared and reappeared, without this provoking either criticism or alarm.

Jean-Baptiste went to bed early that night. He even discouraged the young woman from downstairs, as gently as he could, without offending her. And yet that morning he had felt an urgent desire to see her, to distract his thoughts and help him dream of a different body. But when evening came, his only thought was to get to sleep as fast as he could, without a bedfellow, or a book, or a thought in his head.

When the telephone rang in the small hours, he knew immediately that it had come at last, the end of marking time, the crisis, and that someone had been killed. Margellon was on the line. A man had had his throat cut on the boulevard Raspail, in the quiet section leading to the Place Denfert. Margellon was on the spot with the team from the 14th *arrondissement*.

'And the circle? What's the circle like?' asked Adamsberg.

'Yes, there's a circle, *commissaire*. Carefully drawn, as if the guy was taking his time. And the words round the edge are the same as always: "Victor, woe's in store, what are you out here for?" That's all I can tell you for now. I'll wait for you here.'

'I'm on my way. Call Danglard. Tell him to get there fast.'

'Is it really necessary to get everyone out?'

'Yes. That's what I want. And stay there yourself as well.'

He had added that so as not to offend Margellon.

Adamsberg had pulled on the first pair of trousers and shirt that came to hand, as Danglard noticed, having arrived at the scene a few minutes before him. Adamsberg's shirt buttons were done up awry, as he realised himself. While looking down at the corpse, the *commissaire* therefore unfastened all the buttons, then did them up again, without seeming the least troubled by the incongruous sight he offered to the local officers standing around on the boulevard Raspail. They watched him in silence. It was three-thirty a.m. As on every occasion when it looked likely that the *commissaire* would be the object of critical comment, Danglard had an urge to defend him against allcomers. But in this case, there was nothing he could do.

So Adamsberg calmly finished buttoning up his shirt, while looking at a body which appeared under the arc lamps even more mutilated than that of Madeleine Châtelain. The throat had been so deeply slashed that the man's head was almost back to front.

Danglard, who was feeling as nauseated as when he had seen Madeleine Châtelain's body, tried not to look. His own throat was his most sensitive spot. The idea of wearing a scarf upset him as if it might strangle him. He didn't like shaving under his chin, either. So he looked the other way, towards the dead man's feet, one of which was pointing to the word 'Victor' and the other towards the word 'woe'. The shoes were classic and well-polished. Danglard's gaze moved up the long body, examining the cut of the grey flannel suit and the ceremonial presence of a waistcoat. An elderly doctor, he guessed.

Adamsberg was scrutinising the corpse from the other side, looking at the old man's throat. The *commissaire*'s mouth was twisted in a grimace of disgust for the hand that had slashed that neck. He was thinking of the stupid drooling dog and nothing else. His colleague from the 14th *arrondissement* approached with outstretched hand.

'*Commissaire* Louviers. We haven't met before, Adamsberg. Nasty circumstances.'

'Yes.'

'I thought it best to alert your sector straight away,' Louviers insisted.

'Thank you. Who is this gentleman?' asked Adamsberg.

'I think he was probably a retired doctor. At any rate he was carrying a medical bag with him. Seventy-two years old. Gérard Pontieux, born in the Indre *département*, height 1 metre 79, and that's all we can say at present, just what's on his ID card.'

'We couldn't have prevented it,' said Adamsberg, shaking his head. 'We just couldn't. A second murder was predictable, but not preventable. All the policemen in Paris wouldn't have been enough to stop it.'

'I know what you're thinking,' said Louviers. 'It's your case after that Châtelain murder in your sector, and the killer hasn't been caught yet. He's struck again. Hard to take, isn't it?'

It was true: that was more or less what Adamsberg had been thinking. He had known that this new murder would happen. But not for a moment had he hoped that he could do anything about it. There are stages in an investigation when all you can do is wait for the irreparable to happen if you are to make any progress. Adamsberg could not feel any guilt. But he felt sorry for this harmless well-dressed elderly man stretched out on the pavement, who had had to pay the price for his own powerlessness.

By dawn, the corpse had been taken away in a police van. Conti had come to take some photographs in the morning light, replacing the photographer from the 14th. Adamsberg, Danglard, Louviers and Margellon all met round a table in the Café Ruthène, which had just opened its shutters. Adamsberg remained silent, disconcerting his bulky colleague from the 14th, who was still taking in the hooded eyes, the lop-sided mouth and the dishevelled hair.

'No point asking the café owners this time,' Danglard remarked. 'This one and the Café des Arts close too early, before ten. The chalk circle man knows where to find a deserted spot. It wasn't far from here that he put the dead cat in a circle in the rue Froidevaux, by the Montparnasse cemetery.'

'That's in our sector,' Louviers reacted. 'You didn't tell us.'

'There wasn't a murder then, or even an incident,' Danglard replied. 'We just had a look out of curiosity. Actually, you're not quite right, because it was one of your men who told us about it in the first place.'

'Ah, that's all right then,' said Louviers, relieved not to have been kept out of the loop.

'Like last time,' Adamsberg was saying from the end of the table, 'this victim is entirely inside the circle. You can't tell whether the circle man was responsible or whether his circle's just been used. Always this ambiguity. Very clever.'

'So?' asked Louviers.

'So nothing. The doctor thinks it happened at about one a.m. A bit late, to my mind,' he concluded after another pause.

'What do you mean?' asked Louviers, who wasn't easily discouraged.

'I mean that's after the last metro.'

Louviers went on looking puzzled. Then Danglard read from his expression that he had given up trying to intervene in the conversation. Adamsberg asked what time it was.

'Coming up to eight-thirty,' said Margellon.

'Go and phone Castreau. I asked him to do some checking at about four-thirty. He should have some results by now. Try and catch him before he goes to bed. Castreau takes sleeping seriously.'

When Margellon returned, he reported that the brief checks so far hadn't produced much in the way of information.

'No, I dare say not,' said Adamsberg, 'but let's have them all the same.'

Margellon read from his notes.

'Dr Pontieux has no record with us. We've already informed his sister, who still lives in the family home in the Indre. She's apparently his only living relative. And she's about eighty years old. The parents were ordinary peasant farmers and Dr Pontieux made good, with a career that seems to have absorbed all his energy. Well, that's what Castreau says,' Margellon remarked in an aside. 'He never married, anyway, according to the concierge in his building. Castreau called her. There were no apparent relationships with women or indeed anything remarkable about him, or so Castreau says. He'd lived at that address for the last thirty years, with the surgery on the third floor and his private apartment on the second, and the concierge has known him all that time. She says he was a kind, considerate man, as good as gold, and she was in floods of tears. Verdict: no clouds on the horizon. A sober citizen. An uneventful and boring life. At least—'

'Yes, that's what Castreau says,' Danglard interrupted.

'Does the concierge know why the doctor was out last night?'

'He was called out to a child with a high temperature. He wasn't really practising any more, but some of his former patients still asked for his opinion. He liked going on foot, to get some exercise, obviously.'

'Nothing very obvious about that,' said Adamsberg.

'Anything else?' asked Danglard.

'Nothing else.' Margellon put his notes away.

'A harmless local GP,' Louviers concluded, 'as blameless as your previous victim. Same scenario, it looks like.'

'But there's one big difference,' Adamsberg remarked. 'A colossal difference.'

The three men looked at him in silence. Adamsberg was scribbling with a burnt match on a corner of the paper tablecloth.

'Don't you see what I mean?' he asked, looking up but without seeking to challenge them.

'I can't see what's so obvious about it,' said Margellon. 'What's the colossal difference?'

'This time,' said Adamsberg, 'it's a man that's been killed.'

The pathologist submitted his full report by the end of the afternoon. He estimated the time of death at about one-thirty. Like Madeleine Châtelain, Dr Gérard Pontieux had been knocked unconscious before having his throat cut. The murderer had made a violent assault, slashing the throat at least six times, and cutting through to the vertebrae. Adamsberg winced. The day-long investigation had turned up no more helpful information than they already possessed. They now knew various things about the elderly doctor, but nothing marked him as out of the ordinary. His apartment, his surgery and his private papers had revealed a life without any apparently secret compartments. The doctor had been preparing to rent out his Paris flat and return to his roots in the Indre *département* where he had recently bought a small house, in perfectly normal circumstances. His will left a tidy but by no means extraordinary sum of money to his sister. Danglard returned at about five. He had been searching the crime scene with three of his men. Adamsberg could see that he was looking pleased, but also that he was in need of a glass of wine.

'We found these in the gutter,' Danglard said, holding out a plastic evidence bag. 'Not far from the body, about twenty metres away. The killer didn't even bother to hide them. He's acting as if he's untouchable, absolutely certain he can move about with impunity. First time I've seen anything like that.'

Adamsberg opened the bag. Inside were two pink rubber gloves, sticky with blood. The sight was repulsive.

'This killer seems to see life quite straightforwardly, doesn't he?' said Danglard. 'He kills his man, wearing these gloves, and then just chucks them into the gutter down the street, as if he was getting rid of waste paper. But there won't be any prints: that's the thing with rubber gloves, you can slip them off without touching them and you can pick them up anywhere. So what does this tell us, except that the murderer is pretty cocky? How many people is he going to kill at this rate?'

'It's Friday today. It's a safe bet there won't be anything over the weekend. I get the impression that the circle man doesn't venture out on Saturdays or Sundays. He keeps to regular habits. And if the murderer is someone different, he'll have to wait as well, until there's another circle. Just out of interest, does Reyer have an alibi for last night?'

'Same as ever. He was in bed asleep. No witness. Everyone in that house was asleep. And there's no concierge to spot them coming and going. There are fewer and fewer concierges every day in Paris – bad news for us.'

'Mathilde Forestier called me just now. She'd heard about the murder on the radio and sounded shocked.'

'So she says,' muttered Danglard.

XIII

THEN NOTHING HAPPENED FOR SEVERAL DAYS. ADAMSBERG started inviting his downstairs neighbour into his bed again. Danglard lapsed into his usual procedures for lazy June afternoons. Only the press was agitating. A dozen or so journalists were working shifts to keep up a presence outside the station.

On the Wednesday, Danglard was the first to crack.

'He's got us where he wants us,' he burst out angrily. 'We can't do anything, there's nothing to find, no evidence. We're hanging about like zombies, waiting for him to invent a new trick for us. Nothing to be done until there's another circle. It's enough to drive you mad. It's enough to drive *me* mad, anyway,' he corrected himself, after glancing over at Adamsberg.

'Tomorrow,' said Adamsberg.

'Tomorrow what?'

'Tomorrow morning, there'll be another circle, Danglard.'

'You're a fortune-teller now, are you?'

'We won't go over this again, we've already talked about it. The chalk circle man has a programme. And, as Vercors-Laury says, he needs to exhibit his thoughts. He won't let a whole week go by without showing up somewhere. Especially since the press is full of stories about him. But if he draws a circle tonight, Danglard, we'd better be afraid that there'll be another murder in the night between Thursday and Friday. This time, we must have as many men out on patrol as possible, at least in the 5th, 6th and 14th *arrondissements*.'

'But why? The killer's under no pressure to hurry. And so far he hasn't shown any sign of it.'

'It's different now. Trust me, Danglard. If the circle man *is* the murderer, and he starts drawing circles again, that's because he means to kill again. But he knows he has to move more quickly now. Three witnesses have already described him, not counting Mathilde Forestier. We'll soon be able to construct an identikit picture. He's following what we're doing by reading the newspapers. He knows he hasn't got much longer. So he wants to finish what he's started, and he can't hang about any more.'

'And what if the killer isn't the chalk circle man?'

'Doesn't change anything. He can't count on things lasting for ever, either. His circle man, panicking because of the two crimes, put an end to his games earlier than expected. So he has to hurry before the maniac stops drawing.'

'Possible, I suppose,' said Danglard.

'Very possible, *mon vieux*.'

Danglard spent a restless night. How could Adamsberg be waiting so unhurriedly and where did he get his predictions of the future from? He never seemed to be tied down by tedious facts. He read all the files that Danglard had prepared for him on the victims and suspects, but made little comment on them. He was following some vague scent in the air. Why did he appear to think it so significant that the second victim was a man? Because it meant ruling out a sexual motive for the crimes?

That wouldn't surprise Danglard. He had supposed for a long time that someone was using the chalk circle man for some precise purpose. But neither the Châtelain nor the Pontieux murder seemed to have been of particular benefit to anyone. They merely encouraged the idea of a psychopathic serial killer. Was that the reason they would have to wait for another death? But why did Adamsberg keep concentrating on the chalk circle man? And why had he called Danglard 'mon vieux'? Worn out with tossing and turning in bed in the hot June night, Danglard considered the refreshing possibility of going to the kitchen to finish off the wine. In front of the children, he always took care to leave a little in the bottle. But Arlette would notice next morning that he had been at it in the night. Well, it wouldn't be the first time. She would pull a face and say 'Adrien,' (she often called him Adrien) 'you're an old boozer.' But he was hesitating above all because drinking late at night would give him a hellish headache when he woke up, as if he were being scalped and all his joints were being unscrewed, whereas he needed to be in good shape in the morning. In case there was another circle. And to help organise the patrols for the next evening, which would be the night of the crime. It was infuriating to allow himself to be ruled by Adamsberg's vague hunches. But it was easier in the end than fighting against them.

Then the man drew another circle. At the far end of Paris, in a small street, the rue Marietta-Martin in the 16th *arrondissement*. The local police station took some time to let them know. Since their district had seen no blue chalk circles before, the authorities had not been particularly alert to them.

'Why in a new area?' Danglard wondered.

'To show us that after hanging around the Pantheon district, he isn't the kind of man to be enclosed in routine and that, murder or no murder, he's still got his freedom and his power to cover the entire territory of the capital. Or something like that,' Adamsberg murmured.

'Buggering us up,' said Danglard, pressing a finger to his brow.

He hadn't been able to resist after all, the night before: he'd finished the bottle and had even started another. The iron bar that now seemed to be hammering the inside of his head had almost deprived him of his eyesight. And the most worrying thing of all was that Arlette had said nothing at breakfast. But Arlette knew that he had worries at present, what with his almost empty bank account, the impossible investigation he was engaged in, and the unsettling character of his new boss. Perhaps she didn't want to upset him any further. But that meant that she hadn't realised that Danglard actually liked to hear her say 'Adrien, you're an old boozer.' Because at that moment, he was certain of being loved. A simple but genuine sensation.

In the middle of the circle, this time drawn in a single move-ment, there lay a red plastic object: the rose of a watering can.

'It must have fallen from the balcony up there,' said Danglard, looking up. 'Goes back to the ark, this kind of rose. And why choose it anyway, and not that cigarette packet, for instance?'

'You've seen the list, Danglard. He takes care to pick objects that won't blow away. No metro tickets, paper handkerchiefs, or cellophane wrappers, anything the wind could carry off in the night. He wants to be sure that the thing in the circle will still be there next morning. Which makes me think he's more concerned with the image of himself he's projecting than with "revitalising inanimate objects", as Vercors-Laury would have it. Otherwise he wouldn't rule out flimsy items that are just as significant as any he's used if he's really concerned with the "metaphorical renaissance of the pavement". But the way the chalk circle man looks at it, a circle found empty in the morning would be an insult to his creativity.'

'This time,' Danglard said, 'there'll be no witnesses. It's a quiet spot with no cinema or café that might be open late. People go to bed early round here. He's becoming more discreet now, the circle man.'

For the rest of the morning, Danglard tried to stay quietly applying pressure to his head. After lunch, he felt a little better. He was able to spend all afternoon with Adamsberg organising the extra officers who were being asked to patrol Paris that night. Danglard shook his head, wondering what the point of all this was. But he recognised that Adamsberg had been right about that morning's circle.

By about eight o'clock, everything was in position. The area of the city was so immense, of course, that the network of surveillance was stretched very wide.

'If he's cunning,' Adamsberg said, 'he'll slip through the mesh, obviously. And we know he's cunning.'

'Given where we are now, perhaps we should keep an eye on Mathilde Forestier's house?' Danglard suggested.

'Yes,' Adamsberg replied, 'but for heaven's sake have the surveillance people stay out of sight.'

He waited for Danglard to leave the room before he called Mathilde. He simply asked her to stay in that evening and on no account to try any escapades or to follow anyone.

'Just do me a favour,' he said. 'Don't try to understand. Is Reyer home?'

'Probably,' said Mathilde. 'I'm not his keeper, I don't watch his comings and goings.'

'And Clémence?'

'No, as usual Clémence went trotting off to meet one of her lonely hearts. It never comes to anything. Either she sits waiting in a café for someone who doesn't turn up, or else the minute the guy sees her he pushes off fast. Either way, she gets back in tears. It's completely ridiculous. She shouldn't do this sort of thing in the evening, it just depresses her.'

'OK. Just stay at home till tomorrow, Madame Forestier.'

'Are you afraid that something's going to happen?'

'I don't know,' Adamsberg replied.

'As per usual,' said Mathilde.

Adamsberg decided to stay in the station overnight. Danglard chose to stay with him. The *commissaire* was silently scribbling away, with a pad on his knee, his legs outstretched and resting on the waste-paper basket. Danglard was chewing at some ancient toffees he'd found in Florence's desk, to try to stop himself drinking.

A uniformed policeman was walking up and down the boulevard du Port-Royal beween the little station building at the top of the boulevard Saint-Michel, and the corner of the rue

Bertholet. His colleague was doing the same thing from the Gobelins end.

Since ten that evening, he had paced up and down his beat eleven times and couldn't stop himself counting, although it annoyed him. But what else was there to do? For an hour now, there had been few passers-by on the boulevard. It was early July and Paris was starting to empty for the holidays.

Just then a young woman in a leather jacket went past, walking a little uncertainly. She had a pretty face and was probably on her way home. It was about quarter past one, and the policeman wanted to tell her to hurry up. She looked vulnerable, and he felt concerned for her. He ran after her.

'Mademoiselle, are you going far?'

'No, just to the Raspail metro station.'

'Raspail, oh that's a bit far,' the policeman said. 'Perhaps I'll just see you down the street. There isn't another man on duty before Vavin.'

The girl had short bobbed hair. Her jawline was clear and attractive. No, he certainly didn't want anyone to touch that throat. But this girl looked quite untroubled. She seemed perfectly at home in the city by night.

The girl lit a cigarette. She didn't seem too comfortable in his company.

'What is it? Is something happening?' she asked.

'Apparently it's not safe tonight. I'll just walk you some of the way.'

'If you like,' she replied. But it was clear that she would have preferred to be alone and they walked along in silence.

A few minutes later, the policeman left her at the corner and came back towards the little Port-Royal station. He started off back along the boulevard towards the rue Bertholet.

Twelfth time. By talking to the young woman and walking along with her, he'd lost about ten minutes. But it seemed to him that was part of his job.

Ten minutes. But it had been enough. As he glanced down the length of the rue Bertholet, he saw a long shape on the pavement.

Oh no, he thought despairingly. My bad luck.

He broke into a run. Perhaps it was just a roll of carpet. But no, a stream of blood was trickling towards him. He touched the arm outstretched on the ground. Still warm. It must have just happened. A woman.

His radio crackled. He contacted his colleagues at the Gobelins, Vavin, Saint-Jacques, Cochin, Raspail and Denfert, asking them to pass the news on, not to leave their post and to stop anyone they saw. But if the murderer had been in a car, for instance, he would have got away. The policeman didn't feel guilty for having left his beat to accompany the young woman. Possibly he had saved the life of the girl with the beautiful jawline.

But he hadn't been able to save this woman. Sometimes a life could hang by a thread. There was nothing of the victim's jawline to see. Standing there alone, and feeling revolted, the policeman directed his torch away from the corpse, alerted his superiors and waited, his hand on his pistol. It had been a long time since he had been so distressed by the night.

When the phone rang, Adamsberg looked up at Danglard but didn't give a start.

'Here we go,' he said.

Picking up the telephone, he bit his lip.

'Where? Say that again,' he said after a minute. 'Rue Bertholet? But the 5th should be crawling with men. There should have been four along the boulevard Port-Royal alone. What the devil's happened?'

Adamsberg's voice had risen in pitch. He plugged in the earpiece so that Danglard could hear what the young policeman was saying.

'There were just the two of us on Port-Royal, sir. There was an accident at the Bonne-Nouvelle metro, two trains collided at about eleven-fifteen. No serious casualties, but we had to send some men over.'

'But they should have taken men from the outer districts and sent more to the 5th! I gave explicit instructions that the 5th was to be closely patrolled! I ordered it!'

'Sorry, sir, I can't do anything about that. I didn't get any instructions.'

It was the first time that Danglard had seen Adamsberg almost beside himself with rage. It was true that they had heard about the accident at Bonne-Nouvelle, but both of them had assumed that nobody would be called away from the 5th or the 14th. Some counter-order must have gone out, or perhaps the network Adamsberg had asked for had not been thought so indispensable by someone higher up.

'Well, anyway,' said Adamsberg, with a shake of his head, 'he would have struck, sooner or later. In this street or that, he'd have managed to do it in the end. This man's a monster. We couldn't have prevented it – no use getting worked up. Come on, Danglard, we'd better get over there.'

Over there they found flashing lights, arc lamps, a stretcher, and the police doctor, all for the third time surrounding a body whose throat had been cut, lying inside a blue chalk circle.

'Victor, woe's in store . . .' muttered Adamsberg.

He looked at the latest victim.

'Slashed as viciously as the other one,' the doctor said. 'The killer really went for the cervical vertebrae. The weapon wasn't sharp enough to cut through them, but that was the intention.'

'OK, doc, put it all in writing for us,' said Adamsberg, who could see sweat breaking out on Danglard's face. 'And it wasn't long ago, you reckon?'

'That's right, between about five past one and one thirty-five, if the officer is correct about his beat.'

'And your beat,' said Adamsberg, turning to the constable, 'was from here to the Place du Port-Royal?'

'Yes, sir.'

'What happened? You can't have taken more than twenty minutes to go there and back.'

'No, sir, that's right. But this girl came past, all on her own, just as I was getting up to the station building for the eleventh time. I don't know, call it a foreboding, I thought I'd better see her along to the next corner. It wasn't far. I was in sight of Port-Royal all the way. I'm not trying to excuse myself, *commissaire*, I'm prepared to take responsibility for not sticking to the orders.'

'Forget it,' said Adamsberg. 'He'd have struck anyway. Did you see anyone corresponding to the description we've put out?'

'No, nobody.'

'What about the other officers in the sector?'

'They haven't reported anything.'

Adamsberg sighed.

'See this circle, *commissaire*,' said Danglard. 'It isn't round. That's extraordinary, it isn't circular. The pavement was too narrow here, so he's drawn an oval.'

'Yes, and that must have vexed him.'

'So why didn't he do it on the boulevard where he had plenty of room?'

'Too many policemen hanging about there, Danglard, all the same. So who is this lady?'

Once more, they had to read identity papers by the light of the arc lamps, having found them in her handbag.

'Delphine Le Nermord, *née* Vitruel, age fifty-four. And here's her photo, I think,' said Danglard, who was carefully transferring the contents of the handbag into a plastic evidence bag. 'She looks quite pretty, bit too much make-up. The man holding her shoulder must be her husband.'

'No,' said Adamsberg. 'Can't be. He's not wearing a wedding ring, but she is. Perhaps a lover – he looks younger, too. That might explain why she had the photo on her.'

'Yes, I should have noticed that.'

'It's dark here. Come on, Danglard, we'll get in the van.'

Adamsberg knew that Danglard couldn't face the sight of a cut throat any longer.

They sat down opposite each other on the seats of the police van. Adamsberg started leafing through a fashion magazine from Madame Le Nermord's bag.

'I know that name from somewhere,' he said, 'Le Nermord. But I've got a terrible memory. Have a look in the address book to see if it's got her husband's first name and address.'

Danglard pulled out a dog-eared business card.

'Augustin-Louis Le Nermord. Two addresses. One's the Collège de France, and the other's rue d'Aumale in the 9th.'

'I should recognise the name, but I can't think why.'

'I know who he is,' said Danglard. 'Some time back there was talk of him for a seat in the Academy of Inscriptions and Belles-Lettres. He's a specialist on Byzantium,' he went on, after thinking for a moment. 'An expert on the emperor Justinian.'

'How the hell do you know all that?' asked Adamsberg, lifting his gaze from the magazine in genuine astonishment.

'Well, let's just say I know a bit about Byzantium.'

'But why?'

'I just like knowing stuff, that's all.'

'And the emperor Justinian's empire, you know about that too?'

''Fraid so,' sighed Danglard.

'So when was Justinian?'

Adamsberg was never embarrassed about asking when he didn't know something, even when it was something he should have known.

'Sixth century.'

'BC or AD?'

'AD.'

'This man interests me. Come on, Danglard, we're going to tell him his wife's been killed. Now that one of our victims has a near relative in Paris, we can at least see how he reacts.'

Louis-Augustin Le Nermord's reaction was very simple. Still bleary-eyed from sleep, on hearing what they had to say the diminutive scholar shut his eyes, put his hands on his stomach and went very white about the lips. He dashed from the room, and Danglard and Adamsberg heard him retching somewhere else in the house.

'Well, at least that's clear enough,' said Danglard. 'He's in shock.'

'Unless he took something to make him throw up when he heard the entryphone.'

The man returned, walking gingerly. He had put on a grey dressing-gown over his pyjamas and had evidently doused his head under a tap.

'We're extremely sorry to bring you this news,' said Adamsberg. 'If you would prefer us to ask our questions tomorrow ...'

'No ... no. Please go ahead, messieurs. I'm listening.'

The little man was trying to maintain his dignity, Danglard noted, and he was succeeding. His posture was upright, his brow large, and his cloudy blue eyes were steadfastly fixed on Adamsberg's face. He asked them whether they would mind if he lit his pipe and did so, saying that he needed it.

The light was dim and the pipe smoke heavy in the book-lined room.

'You study Byzantium?' said Adamsberg, with a glance at Danglard.

'Er, yes, I do,' said Le Nermord, looking slightly surprised. 'How did you know?'

'I didn't. But my colleague here recognised your name.'

'That is kind of you to say so. But please, tell me about *her*. What happened, how did it happen?'

'We'll give you more details when you're feeling a bit stronger and better able to hear them. It's already bad enough to find out that she's been murdered. We found her lying inside a blue chalk circle in the rue Bertholet, in the 5th *arrondissement*. Quite a long way from here.'

Le Nermord nodded. His features semed to lose definition. He was looking older already. It was painful to see.

'"Victor, woe's in store, what are you waiting for?" Is that it?' he said in an undertone.

'Not exactly, but near enough,' said Adamsberg. 'So you know about the chalk circle man?'

'Who doesn't? Doing remote historical research doesn't shield you from contemporary life, monsieur, even if you'd like it to. But I can't believe this – I was talking about this maniac with Delphie, that's Delphine, my wife, only last week.'

'Why did you talk about him?'

'Delphie was inclined to defend him, but I felt nothing but disgust for him. Some ghastly joker. But women don't see that.'

'It's a long way from here, the rue Bertholet. Was your wife visiting friends?' Adamsberg continued.

The man thought for a long while, at least five or six minutes. Danglard wondered whether he had really heard the question or whether he was going to fall asleep again. But Adamsberg signalled to him to wait.

Le Nermord struck a match to relight his pipe.

'Far from where?' he asked in the end.

'Well, far from home,' said Adamsberg.

'No, on the contrary, it's quite near where she lives. Delphie lives . . . lived . . . on the boulevard du Montparnasse, near Port-Royal. Do I need to say more about that?'

'Yes, please.'

'She left me nearly two years ago to go and live with her lover. He's a pathetic, stupid, insignificant character, but of course you won't believe that, coming from me. You can judge for yourselves if you see him. It's been upsetting, that's all I can say. And now I live in this barn of a place on my own. Like a fool,' he said waving his arm at the room.

Danglard seemed to hear a catch in his voice.

'But you still used to see her?'

'It was very hard to try and do without her,' answered Le Nermord.

'You were jealous?' asked Danglard, without trying to be tactful.

Le Nermord shrugged.

'Well, monsieur, you get used to anything in the end. I should say that Delphie had been unfaithful to me for twelve years on and off, with a series of lovers. I didn't like it, of course, but I'd given up arguing. In the end you don't know whether it's self-esteem or love that makes you angry, but the anger dies down eventually, and you end up meeting for lunch now and again – we talk politely, and it's sad. I'm sure you know this kind of situation by heart, messieurs, I won't spell out the story of my life. Delphie was no better than she should have been, and I was no hero. I didn't want to lose her for ever. So I had to accept her rules. I confess that I couldn't stand her latest lover, the stupid one. As if she was doing it on purpose, it was the worst of the lot that she was keenest on, so that was when she decided to move out permanently.'

He raised his arms and let them fall on his thighs.

'So,' he said. 'That's it, really. And now it's over.'

He closed his eyes tight, and stuffed his pipe with more tobacco.

'You'll have to provide us with a statement about your movements this evening. That is indispensable, I'm afraid,' said Danglard, as usual not beating about the bush. Le Nermord looked at them in turn.

'I don't understand. You mean it wasn't this lunatic killer who . . .'

'We don't know who it was,' said Danglard.

'Oh, no, messieurs, you've got it wrong. All that comes to me from my wife's death is a hole in my life, desolation. As far as money goes, since I'm sure you'll be interested in that, most of her money, and she had quite a bit, goes to her sister, and indeed so does this house. Delphie had decided that was what she wanted to do. Her sister's always been hard up.'

'Nevertheless,' Danglard repeated, 'we still need an account of your movements. Please.'

'Well, as you saw, there's an entryphone in this house and no concierge. So who could tell you whether I'm telling the truth or not? But . . . well, until about eleven, I was planning my lectures for next year. You can look, they're in that stack of paper on the table. Then I went to bed, read for a while, and went to sleep until I heard the buzzer. But nobody can confirm any of that, can they?'

'More's the pity,' said Danglard.

Adamsberg was letting him run the interview now. Danglard was better than him at putting routine but upsetting questions. Throughout their exchange, he kept his gaze on Le Nermord, who was sitting opposite him.

'Yes, I see,' said Le Nermord, rubbing the warm bowl of the pipe against his forehead, in visible distress. 'I do see. A husband betrayed and humiliated, the new lover who stole away his wife. I understand there are these classic scenarios. Oh God! But do you always have to go for the most obvious solutions? Don't you ever think there could be more complicated explanations?'

170

'Yes,' said Danglard, 'we do sometimes. But I have to say that your situation appears to be delicate.'

'I appreciate that,' agreed Le Nermord. 'I just hope for my own sake that I'm not going to pay the price for any errors of judgement by the police. I suppose this means you want to see me again?'

'On Monday?' suggested Adamsberg.

'Yes, all right, Monday. I suppose, as well, that there's nothing I can do for Delphie now? You're holding her.'

'I'm afraid so, monsieur. Sorry.'

'Will there be a post-mortem?'

'Yes, I'm afraid so.'

Danglard let a minute pass. He always let a minute pass after any reference to a post-mortem.

'For Monday,' he went on, 'please think about what you were doing on Wednesday 19 and Thursday 27 June. Those were the nights of the two previous murders. You'll be asked that. Unless you can tell us now.'

'No need to think,' said Le Nermord. 'It's quite simple and sad. I don't go out at night. I spend every evening writing. Nobody lives with me to confirm that, and I don't see much of my neighbours.'

They all sat nodding, without knowing why. There are moments when everyone just sits nodding.

There was no more to be done that night. Adamsberg, seeing the weariness in the eyes of the scholar of Byzantium, gave the sign that the interview was over, getting up quietly.

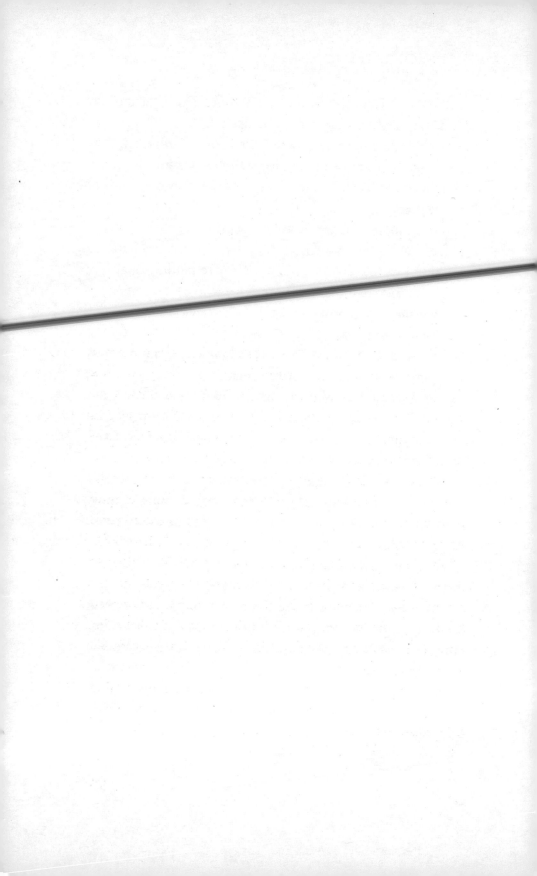

XIV

DANGLARD LEFT HOME NEXT MORNING WITH A BOOK BY Le Nermord under his arm: *Ideology and Society under Justinian*, published eleven years earlier. It was the only one he could find on his shelves. On the back cover there was a short and flattering biography of the author, accompanied by a photograph. A younger Le Nermord was smiling at the camera. He was no better-looking than at present, without any particularly remarkable features – unless you counted regular teeth. The day before, Danglard had noticed that like most pipe-smokers Le Nermord had a tic of tapping the stem against his teeth. A banal remark, as Charles Reyer would have said.

Adamsberg wasn't there. He must already have gone to interview Delphie's lover. Danglard put the book on the *commissaire*'s desk, conscious that he was hoping to impress his boss with the contents of his personal bookshelves. Pointlessly, since he now knew that very few things impressed Adamsberg. Too bad.

Danglard had one aim in his head this morning: to find out what had happened at Mathilde's house during the night. Margellon, who was good at surviving night watches, was waiting for him, ready with his report before going home to bed.

'There were a few comings and goings,' Margellon said. 'I stayed opposite the house until seven-thirty this morning as agreed. The Fish Lady didn't go out. She put the lights off in her sitting room at about half past midnight and her bedroom light about half an hour after that. But that old Valmont creature came staggering in at five past three. She reeked of drink, the works. When I asked what had happened, she started snivelling. Pathetic old bag, isn't she. Anyway, I gathered she'd been waiting all evening for her date – well, she called him her fiancé – to turn up in some bar. He didn't come, so she drank to cheer herself up and passed out at the table. The barman woke her up to chuck her out at closing time. I think she was ashamed, but she was too drunk to stop talking. I couldn't get the name of the bar. It was hard enough getting any sense out of her. And anyway, she gives me the creeps. I helped her as far as the door and left her to sort herself out. Then this morning, out she trots with her little suitcase. She recognised me right away, didn't seem surprised, and told me she was "fed up with trying newspaper ads" and was going off for a few days in the country with some pal of hers, a dressmaker in the Berry. Dressmaking, that's a safer bet, she said.'

'What about Reyer? Did he go out?'

'Yes, he did. He went out dressed up to the nines at about eleven, and came back looking just as spruce, tapping his stick, at one-thirty. I could talk to Clémence because she doesn't know me, but that's not on with Reyer, because he knows my voice. So I stayed undercover and just noted the times. In any case, no way he'd have spotted me, would he?'

Margellon laughed. Yes, he was silly, Danglard thought.

'Call him on the phone for me, Margellon.'

'Who, Reyer?'

'Yes, of course Reyer.'

Charles chuckled when he heard Danglard's voice, though Danglard failed to see why.

'Ha, well now,' said Charles, 'the radio says you've got another problem on your hands, *Inspecteur* Danglard. Brilliant! And you're still harassing me? No other leads in the case?'

'Where did you go last night, Reyer?'

'I went out to see if I could pick up a girl, *inspecteur*.'

'Where?'

'At the *Nouveau Palais*.'

'Can anyone back that up for you?'

'Nope! Too many people in these nightclubs for anyone to remember faces, you must know that.'

'What's so funny, Reyer?'

'You! Your phone call. Makes me laugh. My dear Mathilde, who can't keep her mouth shut, informed me that your *commissaire* told her to be sure and stay in last night. I guessed from that that you thought something might happen. So I decided it was an excellent moment to go out.'

'Why the hell did you have to do that? Do you think it makes my life any easier?'

'That wasn't what I had in mind at all, *inspecteur*. You've been buggering *me* about since the start of this business. I thought it was my turn to have a go.'

'Right. So in fact you went out just to bugger us up?'

'Pretty much, yes, because I didn't manage to pick up any

girls. But I'm glad to learn you're buggered up. *Very* glad – got that?'

'But why?' Danglard asked once more.

'Because it's being so cheerful that keeps me going.'

Danglard hung up, feeling furious. Apart from Mathilde Forestier, nobody had stayed put in the house in the rue des Patriarches the previous night. He sent Margellon home and tackled Delphine Le Nermord's will. He wanted to check what she had left her sister. Two hours later, he had learned that there didn't seem to be a will, at least not in writing. There are days like that when you can't pin anything down.

Danglard paced up and down in his office and thought once more about how the fucking sun was going to explode in four or five billion years, and he didn't know why but that always depressed him. He would have given his life to be sure that the sun would still be shining in five billion years.

Adamsberg returned at about midday and suggested going out for lunch. This didn't happen often.

'Well, it's not looking at all good for our Byzantine expert,' Danglard said. 'He was wrong about the inheritance, or else he was lying. There's no written will. So it all goes to the husband. There are some shares, some forest land, and four houses in Paris, besides the one he lives in. He doesn't have any capital, just his professor's salary and royalties from his books. So if the wife was thinking of divorcing him, all that property would go to someone else.'

'Yes, that's right, she was, Danglard. I met the lover. He's the guy in the photo, all right. It's true that he's built like Tarzan, but he doesn't have an awful lot upstairs. He's a herbivore, what's more, and proud of it.'

'Vegetarian, I suppose you mean,' suggested Danglard.

'All right, yes, vegetarian. He runs an advertising agency with his brother, he's a vegetarian too. They were working together last night until two in the morning, round at the brother's. The brother confirms it. So the lover's in the clear – unless of course the brother's lying. But the lover does seem very upset at Delphine's death. He was pressing her to divorce, not that Le Nermord bothered *him*, but to rescue Delphine from what he called her husband's tyranny. Apparently Augustin-Louis was still getting her to work for him, typing and proof-reading his manuscripts, and filing his notes, and she didn't dare say no. She claimed that she didn't mind, because "it gave her brain a bit of exercise", but the lover thinks it wasn't really what she wanted, and that she was scared stiff of her husband. But Delphine had practically decided to ask for a divorce. At least, she wanted to discuss it with Augustin-Louis. We don't know whether she did or not. Well, it's clear enough that the two men hate each other. The lover would like to see Le Nermord come a cropper.'

'It could all be true, though,' said Danglard.

'Yes, I agree.'

'Le Nermord hasn't got an alibi for any of the nights of the murders. If he wanted to get rid of his wife before she tried to break free, he might have seized the opportunity given him by the chalk circle man. He's not brave, he told us that. Not the type to take a risk. So in order to incriminate the madman, he murders two people at random to make it look like a serial killer, then he kills his wife. All sorted. The cops go after the circle man, and he gets his wife's money.'

'It looks a bit obvious, though, doesn't it? Does he take the police for idiots?'

'For one thing, there are as many idiots in the police as anywhere else. And for another, someone of limited intelligence might come up with an idea like that. I agree, he doesn't look like someone of limited intelligence. But clever people can sometimes act stupid. It happens. Especially when the passions are involved. What about Delphine Le Nermord, though? What was she doing out at night?'

'The lover says she was supposed to be home all evening. When he got in, late, he was surprised not to find her there. He thought perhaps she had gone for cigarettes to a late-night tobacconist in the rue Bertholet, because she often nipped out like that. Then, later, he thought perhaps her husband had called her over to do something for him, yet again. But he didn't dare phone Le Nermord, so he went to bed. I woke him up when I went round there this morning.'

'Le Nermord could have found the circle at about midnight. He could have telephoned his wife, and then cut her throat there. I think Le Nermord's looking very bad. What do you think?'

Adamsberg was scattering breadcrumbs round his plate. Danglard, who was a careful eater, found this irritating.

'What do I think?' said Adamsberg, raising his head. 'I'm thinking about the chalk circle man. You should be starting to guess that by now, Danglard.'

XV

AUGUSTIN-LOUIS LE NERMORD WAS BEING HELD FOR QUESTIONING, starting on the Monday morning. Danglard had made it very plain to him that he was regarded as a prime suspect.

Adamsberg let Danglard handle the questions: Danglard pursued his course mercilessly. The old man seemed incapable of defending himself. Anything he said was immediately pounced on by Danglard's incisive objections. But it was also clear to Adamsberg that Danglard had some sympathy for his victim.

Adamsberg felt nothing of the kind. He had taken an instant dislike to Le Nermord, and he certainly didn't want Danglard to ask him why. So he said nothing.

Danglard kept the questions going for several days.

From time to time, Adamsberg would go into Danglard's office and watch. Driven into a corner, frightened to death by the accusations against him, the old man was visibly falling to pieces. He couldn't even reply to the simplest questions. No, he didn't know that Delphie had never made a written will. He had always thought everything would go to her sister Claire. He was fond of Claire, she was on her own with three children and had a hard life. No, he didn't know what he had been doing on the nights of the murders. He supposed he had been working, then had gone to bed, as he did every night. Danglard contradicted him icily. On the night Madeleine Châtelain had been killed, the local pharmacist had been open late, since it was her turn on the rota. She had seen him going out. Le Nermord explained that yes, that was possible, because he sometimes went out for cigarettes from the machine: 'I take the paper off and use the tobacco in my pipe. Delphie and I both smoked a lot. She was trying to give it up, but I wasn't. I was too lonely in that big house.'

And he would gesture helplessly, and collapse in a heap, while trying all the same to maintain some presence. Not much was left of the eminent professor at the Collège de France, just an old man who seemed at his wits' end, who was desperately trying to fight off an apparently inevitable condemnation. A thousand times or more he repeated: 'But how could it have been me? I *loved* Delphie.'

Danglard, increasingly shaken himself, kept up his barrage, sparing Le Nermord none of the small details which incriminated him. He had even allowed some information to leak out to the press, which had headlined it. The old man had hardly touched any of the food he was brought, in spite of encouragement from Margellon, who could be kind-hearted when he wanted to be. Le Nermord had not shaved either, even when he was allowed home overnight. What astonished Adamsberg was the sudden capitulation of this old man, who must after all have had a good enough brain with which to defend himself. He had never seen such a rapid destabilisation.

By the Thursday morning Le Nermord's legs were genuinely

shaking and he was in a pitiful state. The prosecuting magistrate had asked for him to be charged, and Danglard had just told him of the decision. At this point, Le Nermord said nothing for a long time, just as he had the other night in his house, seeming to weigh up arguments for and against. As before, Adamsberg signalled to Danglard above all not to intervene.

Then Le Nermord said:

'Give me a piece of chalk. Blue chalk.'

Since nobody moved, he found a little authority from somewhere and added:

'Come on. I asked for some chalk.'

Danglard went out and found some in Florence's desk – a repository for everything.

Le Nermord got up with all the precautions of an invalid and took the chalk. Standing against the white wall, he took some time to think again. Then very quickly, he wrote in large letters: *'Victor, woe's in store, what are you out here for?'*

Adamsberg did not move a muscle. He had been expecting this since the previous day.

'Danglard,' he said, 'go and get Meunier. I think he's around somewhere.'

While Danglard left the room, the chalk circle man turned to Adamsberg, determined to look him in the face.

'Well met at last,' said Adamsberg. 'I've been looking for *you* for a long time.'

Le Nermord did not reply. Adamsberg looked at his unattractive face, which had regained a little firmness since this confession.

Meunier, the handwriting specialist, followed Danglard into the room. He considered the large writing which covered the entire length of the wall.

'Nice souvenir for your office, Danglard,' he murmured. 'Yes, that's the writing. It couldn't be imitated.'

'Thank you,' said the chalk circle man, handing the chalk back to Danglard. 'I can fetch more proof if you want it. My notebooks, the times when I went out, and my street map, which is covered with crosses, my list of objects. Anything you like. I know I'm asking too much, but would it be possible for this to be kept quiet? I would dearly like it if my students and colleagues didn't find out. But I imagine that's not possible. Still, it puts a different complexion on things, doesn't it?'

'Yes, I suppose so,' Danglard admitted.

Le Nermord got up, finding more strength, and accepted a glass of beer. He paced from the window to the door, going to and fro in front of his line of graffiti.

'I had no choice, I had to tell you. There was too much evidence piling up against me. But now I've told you, it alters things, doesn't it? Do you think that if I'd really wanted to kill my wife, I'd have done it in one of my own circles? Without even bothering to disguise my handwriting? I hope we can please agree about that, at least.'

He shrugged his shoulders.

'Of course, there's no point now in hoping to be elected to the Academy. Or preparing my lectures for next year. The Collège won't want to have anything to do with me after this. Perfectly understandable. But I didn't have any choice. I had to go for the lesser of two evils, because the murder charge was so serious. It's up to you to find out what's really been happening. Who's been using me? Ever since the first murder victim was found in one of my circles, I've been trying to understand – I felt I'd been caught in some sort of ghastly trap. I was very frightened when I heard about that first murder. As I told you, I'm not a brave man. In fact, frankly, I'm a coward. I racked my brain trying to understand. Who could have done it? Who'd been following me? Who'd put that woman's body in my circle? And if I went on drawing circles after that, it wasn't, as the press said, to tease the police. No, not at all. It was in the hope of finding out who was dogging my steps, who was the murderer, and to give myself some chance of proving my own innocence. I took a few days to reach that decision. You don't easily decide to tempt a murderer to follow you at night, especially if you're as cowardly as me. But I thought that once you found out who *I* was, I'd certainly be accused of murder. And that's what the murderer must have been thinking: he was hoping that *I'd* pay for *his* crimes. So it was a sort of struggle between him and me. The first real struggle I'd had in my life. And in that sense, I don't regret it. But the only thing I didn't for a moment imagine was that he would attack my own wife. All night, after you came to see me, I sat up asking myself why he had done that. I could think of only one explanation. The police had still not identified me with the circles, and that was spoiling the murderer's plans. So he did this, he murdered my own Delphie, so that you'd come straight to me, and then he would be left in peace. Am I right?'

'It's possible,' said Adamsberg.

'But he was mistaken in one thing: any of your shrinks will tell you that I'm perfectly sane, I haven't lost my mind. I suppose a lunatic might kill two strangers and then his own wife. But not me. I'm not insane. And I would never have killed Delphie and dragged her into one of my circles. Delphie. If it hadn't been for my damned circles, she'd still be alive.'

'Well, if you're as sane as you say,' asked Danglard, 'why on earth *did* you draw those damned circles?'

'So that lost things would belong to me, would be grateful to me. No, I'm not putting this very well.'

'No, you're not – I don't get it at all,' said Danglard.

'I can't help it,' said Le Nermord. 'I'll try to write it down, that might work better.'

Adamsberg was thinking of Mathilde's description: 'A little man who's lost everything and is greedy for power, how will he get out of this?'

'Please find him,' Le Nermord begged, in distress. 'Find this killer. Do you think you can find him? Really?'

'If you help us,' said Danglard. 'For instance, did you ever see anyone following you when you went out?'

'Nothing clear enough to help you, unfortunately. At the beginning, two or three months ago, this woman sometimes followed me. It was long before any murder, and it didn't bother me. I found her odd, but somehow friendly. I had the feeling that she was encouraging me from a distance. At first I was a bit scared of her, then I got to like seeing her. But what can I say? I think she was fairly tall, dark hair, good-looking and perhaps not young. But I can't give you more detail than that. Still, I'm certain it was a woman.'

'Yes,' said Danglard, 'we know about her. How many times did you see her?'

'About a dozen times.'

'And after the first murder?'

Le Nermord hesitated, as if he didn't wish to remember something.

'Yes,' he said. 'After that I did see someone twice, but it wasn't the dark woman. Someone else. Because I was scared,

I hardly turned to look and ran off once I'd done my circle. I didn't really have the guts to follow through on my plan, which was to try and see the face of the person. It was quite a small figure. Could have been a man or a woman, a peculiar outline. See, I can't help you much.'

'Why did you always have your bag with you?' Adamsberg interrupted.

'My briefcase?' said Nermord. 'With my papers? After I'd drawn my circle, I would go away quickly, usually by metro. I was so nervous that I needed to read, get back to my notes and return to being a professor. I'm sorry, I don't know if I can explain it better than that. What will happen to me now?'

'Well, we'll probably let you go for now,' said Adamsberg. 'The magistrate won't want to risk a false murder charge.'

'No, of course not,' said Danglard. 'This does somewhat change things.'

Le Nermord looked a little better. He asked for a cigarette and packed the tobacco into his pipe.

'It's a pure formality, but I would still like to visit your house, if I may,' said Adamsberg.

Danglard, who had never seen Adamsberg bother to carry out pure formalities, looked at him uncomprehendingly.

'As you wish,' said Le Nermord. 'But what are you looking for? As I said, I'll bring you all the proof you need.'

'Yes, I know. And I'll trust you to do that. I'm not looking for anything concrete. Meanwhile, can you go over all that with Danglard, and make a statement.'

'Can you be frank with me, *commissaire*? As the "chalk circle man", what kind of sentence will I get?'

'I can't think the charge will be serious,' said Adamsberg. 'There was no disturbance, no offence against public order in the strict sense. If you inspired someone with the idea of committing a murder, that's not your fault. You can't be held responsible for giving other people ideas. Your peculiar habit has caused three deaths, but we can hardly blame you for them.'

'I would never have imagined this. I'm truly sorry,' murmured Le Nermord.

Adamsberg went out without another word, and Danglard felt annoyed at him for not having shown a little more humanity. He had previously seen the *commissaire* go to great lengths to be kind, to win over various strangers and even imbeciles. But today he hadn't offered the tiniest crumb of humanity to the old man in front of them.

Next day, Adamsberg asked to see Le Nermord again. Danglard was sulking. He didn't want them to harass the old man any further. And here was Adamsberg choosing the last minute to call him in, when he'd hardly said a word to him the previous days.

So Le Nermord was convoked once more. He came into the police station timidly, still looking shaken and pale. Danglard considered him.

'He's changed,' he whispered to Adamsberg.

'I wouldn't know,' Adamsberg replied.

Le Nermord sat on the edge of a chair and asked if he could smoke his pipe.

'I was thinking, last night,' he said, feeling in his pocket for matches. 'All night, in fact. And now I've decided that I don't care if everyone finds out the truth about me. I'll just have to accept that I'm the pathetic chalk circle man, as the press calls me. At first when I started doing it, I had the feeling that it was making me incredibly powerful. In fact, I suppose, I was being arrogant and grotesque. And then it all went so wrong. Those two murders. And my Delphie. How could I possibly hope to hide all that from myself? What would be the point of trying to hide it from other people, and trying to salvage my career, which I've completely destroyed, however you look at it? No. I was the circle man. If I have to live with that, so be it. Because of all this, because of my "frustration" as that man Vercors-Laury would call it, three people have died. Including my Delphie.'

He plunged his head in his hands and Danglard and Adamsberg waited in silence, without looking at each other. The elderly Le Nermord wiped his eyes with the sleeve of his raincoat, like an old tramp, as if he were abandoning the prestige he had spent years acquiring.

'So it's pointless of me to beg you not to let the press know,' he continued with an effort. 'I get the impression that it would be better if I just accept what I am and what I've done, instead of trying to hide behind my wretched professorial identity. But since I'm a coward, I'd prefer to get away from Paris, now that everything will come out. I meet too many people in the street, you see. If you give me permission, I'd like to retreat to the countryside. Not that I like the countryside. We bought a little house there for Delphie to use. It could be my refuge from the world for now.'

Le Nermord waited for their reply, rubbing the bowl of his pipe against his cheek, an anxious and miserable expression on his face.

'You're quite free to do that,' said Adamsberg, 'so long as you keep us informed of your whereabouts. That's all we will ask.'

'Thank you. I think I could move down there in a couple of weeks. I'm going to clear everything out. Byzantium's finished for me now.'

Adamsberg let another pause go past before he asked:

'You aren't by any chance diabetic, are you?'

'What a strange question, *commissaire*. No, I'm not diabetic. Is that . . . er . . . important?'

'Well, it is quite. I'm going to trouble you again one last time, although it's about something trivial. But this trivial thing is hard to explain, and I hoped you might be able to help me. All the witnesses who saw you have spoken of a smell you left behind. A smell of rotten apples, one said, vinegar or a liqueur of some sort, others said. So I thought at first that you might be suffering from diabetes, since as you may know diabetes is associated with a slight aroma of fermentation. However, I don't detect anything like that about you – just your pipe tobacco. So I thought possibly the smell they spoke of might have come from your clothes, or from a clothes cupboard. And yesterday I looked in your wardrobes and cupboards, and sniffed at the clothes. Nothing. Just a smell of wooden furniture, dry cleaning, pipe tobacco, books, even chalk, but nothing acid or alcoholic. I was disappointed.'

'I don't really know what to say,' said Le Nermord, looking rather disorientated. 'What exactly are you asking me?'

'Well, how do *you* explain it?'

'I don't know! I never realised I left any *smell* behind me. It's rather humiliating, in fact, to learn this.'

'I have a suggestion. Perhaps it comes from outside your house, from some other cupboard where you used to leave the clothes you wore when you were being the circle man.'

'My clothes when I was "being the circle man"? But I didn't wear anything special! I wasn't demented enough to dress up for my outings! No, *commissaire*. Your witnesses will surely have said that I was dressed in ordinary clothes, like I am today. I wear practically the same things every day: flannel trousers, white shirt, tweed jacket, raincoat. I hardly ever dress any differently. Why on earth would I go out wearing a tweed jacket and go "somewhere else" to put on another tweed jacket, especially one that smelled odd?'

'That's exactly what I was wondering.'

Le Nermord was looking miserable again and Danglard felt vexed with Adamsberg once more. In the end the *commissaire* wasn't so bad at torturing his suspects.

'I do want to help you,' said Le Nermord, his voice on the point of breaking, 'but that's asking too much. I don't understand this business of a smell and why it's so interesting.'

'It may not be as interesting as all that.'

'Perhaps, you know, it might have something to do with nervousness, because these circles were a very emotional thing for me. Maybe I was giving off a sort of "smell of fear"? I suppose it's possible. When I was in the metro afterwards, I'd be dripping with sweat.'

'It really doesn't matter,' said Adamsberg, scribbling on the table. 'Forget it. I get these ideas fixed in my head and they don't mean anything. I'll let you go, Monsieur Le Nermord. I hope you find some peace in the countryside. People say it's possible.'

Peace in the countryside indeed! Danglard, infuriated, gave a snort of exasperation. Everything about the *commissaire* was getting on his nerves this morning, his aimless meanderings, his pointless questions and his banal remarks. Oh, for a glass of white wine. Too early, much too early, control yourself for heaven's sake.

Le Nermord gave a tragic smile and Danglard tried to cheer him up a bit by shaking his hand warmly. But Le Nermord's hand remained limp. A lost soul, Danglard thought.

Adamsberg stood up and watched Le Nermord go down the corridor, stooping slightly and looking thinner than ever.

'Poor sod,' said Danglard. 'He's finished now.'

'I'd have preferred it if he *had* been diabetic,' was Adamsberg's only reply.

Adamsberg spent the rest of the morning reading *Ideology and Society under Justinian*. Danglard, feeling almost as exhausted as his victim after the long joust with the chalk circle man, would have liked Adamsberg to stop thinking about him and move the investigation on in some other direction. He felt so saturated with Augustin-Louis Le Nermord that the last thing in the world he wanted to do was read a line he had written. Out of every page, the cloudy blue gaze of the Byzantine scholar would have seemed to stare at him, reproaching him for his persecution.

Danglard came to find Adamsberg at one o'clock. He was still plunged in his book. Danglard remembered that the *commissaire* had told him that he read slowly, one word after another. He did not look up as he heard Danglard come in.

'Do you remember that fashion magazine we found in Madame Le Nermord's handbag, Danglard?'

'The one you were looking at in the van? Must still be in the lab.'

Adamsberg called the lab and asked for the magazine to be sent down if they had finished with it.

'What's bothering you now?' asked Danglard.

'I don't really know. But at least three things are on my mind. The smell of rotten apples, the good doctor Gérard Pontieux, and the fashion magazine.'

Adamsberg called Danglard back in a little later. He was holding a small piece of paper.

'Here's the train timetable,' Adamsberg said. 'There's one leaving in fifty-five minutes for Marcilly, the native heath of our Dr Pontieux.'

'What bothers you about the doctor?'

'He bothers me because he's a man.'

'Still on about that?'

'I told you before, Danglard. My mind works slowly. Do you think you could catch this train?'

'Today? Now?'

'If you would. I want to know everything about this doctor. You'll find some people there who knew him in his younger days, before he set up his practice in Paris. Ask them about him. I want to know all about him. Absolutely everything. We're missing something here.'

'But how can I ask questions if I haven't the slightest idea what you want to know?'

Adamsberg shook his head. 'Just go down there, and question anyone you can. I've every confidence in you. Don't forget to phone me.'

Adamsberg waved to Danglard and, looking absent-minded, went downstairs to find something to eat. He chewed his cold lunch as he made his way over to the National Library.

At the reception desk, his shirtsleeves and worn black canvas trousers did not create the most favourable impression. He showed his card and said he wanted to consult the complete works of Augustin-Louis Le Nermord.

Danglard arrived at Marcilly station at ten past six, just the right time for a glass of white wine at a café table. There were six cafés in Marcilly, and he went round all of them, meeting plenty of old people who remembered Gérard Pontieux. But what they had to say held little interest. He was getting bored with the life of the young Gérard, which had apparently been incident-free. It seemed to him that it would have been more profitable to concentrate on his medical career. You never knew: perhaps an assisted death, or a faulty diagnosis somewhere in the past. Anything could have happened. But that wasn't what Adamsberg was after. The *commissaire* had sent him here, where nobody knew what had become of Pontieux beyond the age of twenty-four.

By ten o'clock, Danglard was dragging himself round Marcilly on his own, light-headed with local wine and having learnt nothing of substance. He didn't want to return empty-handed to Paris. He felt he should keep trying, although spending the night here was not an attractive option. He called the children to wish them goodnight. Then he went to the address that had been given him in the last café, where there was a possible room for the night. His hostess was an old lady who served him yet another glass of the local wine. Danglard felt like pouring out all his woes to this aged but lively face.

XVI

WITHOUT TELLING ANYONE, MATHILDE HAD BEEN FRETTING ALL week. In the first place, she had not been best pleased to hear Charles coming in at half past one in the morning, and then learning next morning that another woman had been murdered. And as if to rub salt in the wound, Charles had spent the evening joking maliciously, in a thoroughly aggravating way. At the end of her tether, she had thrown him out of her apartment and told him he could come back when he was in a better mood. It worried her, there was no disguising it. As for Clémence, she had come back very late the same night in tears, and completely distraught. Mathilde had spent a fruitless hour trying to sort her out. Finally Clémence, her nerves shattered, had agreed that it would do her good to have a change of scene. The lonely-hearts ads were very bad for her. Mathilde had approved of this immediately, and sent her back up to the Stickleback to pack her case and take a few hours' rest. She was cross with herself, because next morning as she heard Clémence tiptoeing downstairs trying not to disturb her, she had thought: 'Good riddance, four days without having to put up with her.' Clémence had promised to come back the following Wednesday to finish the classification she had started. She probably guessed that her friend the dressmaker wouldn't be too keen to keep her longer than that. She was fairly clear-eyed, old Clémence. How old was she, anyway? Mathilde wondered. Sixty, seventy, somewhere in between? Her dark red-rimmed eyes and her unattractive pointed teeth made it difficult to guess.

During the week, Charles had continued to pull his own handsome face into infuriating expressions, and Clémence had failed to return as agreed. The slides were still scattered on the table. Charles was the first to say that it was a bit worrying, but maybe it wouldn't be such a bad thing if the old woman had followed some man she met in the train and got herself murdered. This caused Mathilde to have a nightmare. When the funny little shrew-mouse hadn't returned by Friday evening, she had been on the verge of starting to search for her by calling the dressmaker.

At which point Clémence turned up again. 'Oh shit!' said Charles who was sitting on the sofa in Mathilde's apartment, running his fingers over a book in Braille. But Mathilde was relieved. All the same, looking at them both invading her room, the magnificent-looking man, sprawling on the couch, and the little old woman taking off her nylon overall but keeping her beret on her head, Mathilde told herself that something wasn't right in her house.

XVII

ADAMSBERG LOOKED UP TO SEE DANGLARD ARRIVING IN HIS OFFICE at nine in the morning, a finger pressed to his brow but in a state of high excitement. He flopped down heavily into an armchair and took a few deep breaths.

'Sorry,' he said. 'I've been running. I took the first train back from Marcilly this morning. Couldn't reach you by phone, you weren't home.'

Adamsberg spread his hands in a gesture signifying: 'Can't be helped, you don't always choose which bed you end up in.'

'The lovely old lady I lodged with,' said Danglard in between breaths, 'knew your famous doctor very well. So well, in fact, that he confided in her. I'm not surprised – she's a special kind of woman. Gérard Pontieux had been engaged, she told me, to the daughter of the local pharmacist, a girl who was plain, but rich. He needed money to set up in practice. And then, at the last minute, he felt disgusted with himself. He told himself that if he started out like that, based on a lie, he wouldn't make an honest doctor. So he pulled out and jilted the girl, the day after the engagement had been announced, sending her a cowardly letter telling her that he couldn't go through with it. Well, none of that's so serious, is it? Not serious at all. Except for the girl's name.'

'Clémence Valmont,' said Adamsberg.

'Spot on,' said Danglard.

'We're going over there,' said Adamsberg, stubbing out the cigarette he had just lit.

Twenty minutes later, they were standing at the door of 44 rue des Patriarches. It was Saturday morning and everything seemed quiet. Nobody answered the interphone to Clémence's flat.

'Try Mathilde Forestier,' said Adamsberg, for once almost tense with impatience. 'Jean-Baptiste Adamsberg here,' he said into the interphone. 'Open the street door, Madame Forestier. Be quick, please.'

He ran up the stairs to the Flying Gurnard on the second floor, where Mathilde opened her door.

'I need the key for upstairs, Madame Forestier. Clémence's key. You've got a spare?'

Mathilde went, without asking questions, to fetch a bunch of keys labelled 'Stickleback'.

'I'll come up with you,' she said, her voice even huskier first thing in the morning than in the evening. 'I've been worrying myself silly, Adamsberg.'

They all trooped into Clémence's apartment. Nothing. No sign of life, no clothes in the wardrobe, no papers on the tables.

'Oh, sod it! Bird's flown,' said Danglard.

Adamsberg paced round the room, more slowly than ever, looking at his feet, opening an empty cupboard here, pulling out a drawer there, then pacing round some more. 'He's not thinking about anything,' thought Danglard, feeling exasperated, and especially exasperated at their failure. He would have liked Adamsberg to explode with anger, then to react quickly and dash about giving orders, to try and retrieve this mess one way or the other, but it was no use hoping he would do anything like that. On the contrary, he gave a charming smile as he accepted the coffee offered them by Mathilde, who was distraught.

Adamsberg called the office from her flat, and described Clémence Valmont as precisely as possible.

'Issue this description to all stations, airports, gendarmeries and so on. The usual thing. And send a man over here. The apartment will have to be watched.'

He replaced the phone quietly and drank his coffee calmly as if nothing had happened.

'You need to take it easy – you don't look well,' he said to Mathilde. 'Danglard, try and explain to Madame Forestier what's been happening, as gently as you can. I won't do it myself, you'll have to excuse me. I don't explain things well.'

'You saw in the papers that Le Nermord had been released without charge over the murders, but that he *was* the blue circle man?' Danglard began.

'Yes, of course,' said Mathilde. 'I saw his photo. And yes, that was the man I followed, *and* it was the same man who used to eat in the little restaurant in Pigalle, a few years ago! Harmless! I got tired of telling Adamsberg that. Humiliated, frustrated, anything you like, but harmless. I did tell you, *commissaire!*'

'Yes, you did. But I didn't agree,' said Adamsberg.

'Quite,' said Mathilde with emphasis. 'But where's the poor

old shrew-mouse gone now? Why are you looking for her? She came back from the countryside last night, looking much better, full of beans, so I don't understand why she's gone off again today.'

'Has she ever told you about the fiancé who jilted her long ago without warning?'

'Yes, more or less,' said Mathilde. 'But it didn't affect her that much. You're not going in for crackpot psychology now, are you?'

'We have to,' said Danglard. 'Gérard Pontieux, the second murder victim, that was him. Clémence's long-lost fiancé, from fifty years ago.'

'You can't be serious,' said Mathilde.

'I'm deadly serious, I've just got back from Marcilly,' said Danglard. 'The town they both came from. She wasn't originally from Neuilly, Mathilde.'

Adamsberg noted that Danglard was calling Madame Forestier 'Mathilde'.

'The rage and madness he'd caused her had been festering for fifty years,' Danglard went on. 'So as she was nearing the end of a life that she considered blighted, her thoughts turned to murder. And the chalk circle man offered a unique opportunity. It was now or never. She'd always kept track of Gérard Pontieux, the target of her obsession. She knew where he lived. She left Neuilly to try and find the man who was drawing the circles, and she came to you, Mathilde. You were the only person who could lead her to him. And to his circles. First of all, she killed that poor fat middle-aged woman, who was just someone at random, to start some sort of "series". Then she killed Pontieux. She took such pleasure in the attack that it was really vicious. And then, because she was afraid the investigation wouldn't find the chalk circle man fast enough, and would be looking all the more closely at the murder of the doctor, she decided to attack the circle man's own estranged wife, Delphine Le Nermord. She had to make it look similar to the attack on Pontieux, so that the police doctor wouldn't be able to point out any differences. Except that he was a man.'

Danglard glanced over at Adamsberg, who said nothing, but motioned to him to carry on.

'The last murder led us straight to the circle man, just as she'd foreseen. But Clémence Valmont thinks in peculiar ways – very twisted but naive at the same time. Because for the circle man to be the murderer of his own wife was going too far. Unless he was completely mad, Le Nermord would hardly have chosen to bring the police straight to his door. So eventually, yesterday, we let him go. Clémence hears that on the radio. With Le Nermord off the hook, everything looks different. Her plan bites the dust. She still has time to get away. So that's what she does.'

Mathilde looked from one to the other in consternation. Adamsberg waited for it to sink in. He knew it would take time, and that she would not want to believe it.

'No, that can't be it,' said Mathilde. 'She'd never have had the physical strength. Remember what a skinny little thing she is?'

'There are plenty of ways to get round that,' said Danglard. 'You could pretend to be ill, sitting on the pavement and wait for someone to bend down, then hit them on the head. All the victims had been knocked unconscious first, remember, Mathilde.'

'Yes, I remember,' said Mathilde, distractedly running her

fingers through strands of her dark hair as it fell over her forehead. 'But what about the doctor? How did she catch him?'

'Very simple. She must have arranged to meet him in a certain place.'

'Why would he come?'

'Oh, he would. Someone from your past suddenly calls on your help. You forget, you drop everything and you come running.'

'Yes, of course, you must be right,' said Mathilde.

'The nights of the murders. Was she home? Can you remember?'

'Well, she used to go out just about every night, for these so-called rendezvous, like the other night. Oh damn it all, that was some act she was putting on for me. Why don't you say anything, *commissaire*?'

'I'm trying to think.'

'To any purpose?'

'No. I'm getting nowhere. But I'm used to that.'

Mathilde and Danglard exchanged glances, both looking disappointed. But Danglard was no longer in a mood to criticise Adamsberg. Yes, Clémence had vanished. But all the same, it was Adamsberg who had understood that something wasn't right and had sent Danglard off to Marcilly.

Adamsberg got up without warning, made a nonchalant pointless gesture, thanked Mathilde for the coffee and asked Danglard to have the technical team come and check Clémence Valmont's apartment.

'I'm going for a walk,' he said, so as not to leave without saying anything. Any excuse so as not to hurt their feelings.

Danglard stayed for a while with Mathilde. They couldn't

stop talking about Clémence, trying to understand. The fiancé who abandons you, the cruel procession of lonely-hearts advertisements, neurotic feelings, little pointed teeth, bad impressions, ambiguities. From time to time, Danglard would get up and see how the technicians were getting on upstairs, and come back saying: 'They're in the bathroom now.' Mathilde poured out some more coffee after adding hot water to the pot. Danglard felt comfortable. He would gladly have stayed there for ever with his elbows on the table with its fish swimming under the glass, lit up by Queen Mathilde's dark-skinned face. She asked him about Adamsberg. How had he guessed all this?

'No idea,' said Danglard. 'And yet I've watched him working, or rather not working. He sometimes seems so casual and offhand that you'd think he'd never been a policeman, then at other times his face is all tense and screwed up, so pre-occupied that he doesn't hear a thing you say. But preoccupied by what? That's the question.'

'He doesn't look as if he's satisfied,' Mathilde remarked.

'No, that's true. Because Clémence has done a runner.'

'No, Danglard. I think he's worried about something else.'

One of the technicians, Leclerc, came into the room.

'About the prints, *inspecteur*. None at all. She must have wiped everything, unless she was wearing gloves the whole time. Never seen anything like it. But in the bathroom, I found a drop of dried blood on the wall, down behind the washbasin.'

Danglard ran upstairs behind him.

'She must have washed something. Maybe the rubber gloves, before throwing them away. We didn't find any near Delphine's body. Get it analysed, fast as you can, Leclerc.

If it's blood from Madame Le Nermord, that pins it on Clémence once and for all.'

A few hours later, analysis had confirmed that the blood was that of Delphine Le Nermord. A wanted notice went out for Clémence.

On hearing the news, Adamsberg remained depressed. Danglard thought about the three things that had been on Adamsberg's mind. Number one was Dr Pontieux. Well, that was resolved now. That left the fashion magazine. And the smell of rotten apples. He was certainly fretting about the rotten apples. But what point was there in that now? Danglard reflected that Adamsberg had found a different method from his own for making himself unhappy. In spite of his casual manner, Adamsberg had discovered an effective way of stopping himself finding any rest.

Most of the time, the door between the *commissaire*'s office and Danglard's remained open. Adamsberg didn't need to isolate himself to be alone. So Danglard came and went, put down files, read him a report, went off again or sat down for a brief chat. And now, more often since Clémence's disappearance, Adamsberg didn't seem receptive to anything, but carried on reading without looking up. Not that this hurt Danglard's feelings, since it was obviously unintentional. It was more a kind of absence than a lack of attention, Danglard thought. Because Adamsberg did pay attention. But to what? He had an odd way of reading too, usually standing up, gripping his arms by the elbows and peering down at notes on the table. He could stay like that for hours on end. Danglard, who was aware all day of his body feeling weary and of his legs being unwilling to carry him, wondered how he managed it.

Just then, Adamsberg was standing up, looking at a little notebook with blank pages, open on his desk.

'Sixteen days now,' said Danglard, sitting down.

'Yes,' said Adamsberg.

This time he looked up at Danglard. It was true that there was nothing to read in the notebook.

'It's not normal,' Danglard went on. 'We should have found her by now. She's got to go out, to eat and drink, she must sleep somewhere. And her description's all over the papers. She can't possibly escape. Especially looking the way she does. But there we are. She's managed it somehow.'

'Yes,' said Adamsberg, 'she's managed it. There's something wrong somewhere.'

'I wouldn't put it like that,' said Danglard. 'I'd say we've taken too long to find her, but we will in the end. She's good at keeping a low profile, the old trout. In Neuilly, nobody seems to have known much about her. What do the neighbours say? That she didn't bother anyone, that she was independent, funny-looking, always with her little beret on, and addicted to the lonely-hearts ads. Nothing else. She lived there for twenty years, for heaven's sake, and nobody knows whether she had any friends, nobody knows whether she had another hideaway, and nobody remembers just when she left there. Apparently she never went on holiday. There are people like that who go through life without anyone else taking any notice of them. It's not so strange that she ended up murdering someone. But it's only a matter of time. We'll find her.'

'No, there's something wrong here somewhere.'

'What do you mean?'

'That's just what I'm trying to puzzle out.'

Discouraged, Danglard pulled himself heavily to his feet in three stages – trunk, buttocks, legs – and paced round the room.

'I'd like to try to know what *you*'re trying to know,' he said.

'By the way, Danglard, the lab can have the fashion magazine back now. I've finished.'

'You've finished what?'

Danglard was anxious to get back to his office, and anxious about this discussion which he knew would lead nowhere, but he couldn't prevent himself thinking that Adamsberg had some idea, perhaps some hypothesis, and that alerted his curiosity, even though he suspected that whatever it was had not yet become clear to Adamsberg himself.

The *commissaire* looked back at the notebook.

'This fashion magazine,' he said, 'contained an article signed Delphine Vitruel. That was Delphine Le Nermord's maiden name. The editor told me that she was a regular contributor, writing an article almost every month about what was in fashion, skirt lengths or seams in stockings. And that interested me. I read the whole lot. It took some time. And then there's the smell of rotten apples. I'm starting to understand some things.'

Danglard shook his head. 'What about the rotten apples?' he said. 'We can't arrest Le Nermord for smelling of fear. So why are you still worrying about him, for heaven's sake?'

'Anything small and cruel intrigues me. You've been listening too much to Mathilde. Now you're defending the circle man.'

'I'm doing nothing of the kind. I'm just concerned about Clémence, so I'm leaving him alone.'

'I'm concerned about Clémence too, nothing but Clémence. Doesn't alter the fact that Le Nermord is a creep.'

'*Commissaire*, one should be sparing with one's contempt, because of the large number of those in need of it. I didn't make that up.'

'Who did?'

'Chateaubriand.'

'Him again. Not good for you, is he?'

'No, he isn't. But anyway. Sincerely, *commissaire*, is this circle man such a contemptible person? He's an eminent historian . . .'

'Well, I wouldn't know about that.'

'I give up,' said Danglard, sitting down. 'To each his obsession. Mine's Clémence right now. I've got to find her. She's out there somewhere, and I'm going to run her to ground. It's got to happen. It's logical.'

'Ah,' said Adamsberg, with a smile, 'foolish logic is the demon of weak minds. I didn't make that up either.'

'Who did?'

'The difference between you and me, Danglard, is that I don't know who said it. But I like that quotation, it suits me. Because I'm not logical. I'm off for a walk now. I need it.'

Adamsberg went for a walk until evening. It was the only way he had found to sort out his thoughts. As if, thanks to the exercise, his thoughts were being stirred, like particles in a suspension. That way, the heavier ones fell to the bottom and the more delicate ones floated to the top. In the end, he came to no conclusion, but at least he now had a decanted version of his thoughts, organised by gravity. At the top, there bobbed up and down things like that pathetic character Le Nermord, his retreat from Byzantium, and his habit of tapping his pipe against his teeth, which were not even stained yellow by tobacco. Dentures, obviously. And the rotten-apple smell. And Clémence, the murderer, disappearing with her black beret, her nylon overalls and her red-rimmed eyes.

He froze. In the distance a young woman was hailing a taxi. It was getting late, he couldn't see her very well, and he began to run. But it was too late, a waste of time, the taxi had pulled away. He stood on the pavement, panting. Why had he run? It would have been good just to see Camille get into a taxi, without running after her. Without even trying to catch her.

He clenched his fists in his jacket pockets, feeling a little emotional. Well, that was normal.

Quite normal. Not worth making a fuss about it. If he had seen Camille, been surprised, and run after her, it was perfectly normal to feel a little upset. It was the surprise. Or the speed. Anybody's hands would be trembling the same way.

But was it even her? Probably not. She lived on the other side of the world. And it was absolutely indispensable that she should go on living on the other side of the world. But that profile, that body, the way of holding the car window with both hands to speak to the driver . . . So what? Plenty of people might look like that. Camille is on the other side of the world. No need to discuss it, or to get upset about seeing a girl getting into a taxi.

But what if it was Camille? Well, if it was, he'd missed her. That was all. She was catching a taxi to go back to the other side of the world. No point wondering about it, the situation remained exactly the same as before. Camille vanishing into the night. Appearing. Disappearing.

He went on his way, feeling calmer, and chanting those two words to himself. He wanted to get to sleep quickly, so as to forget Le Nermord's pipe, Clémence's beret and the tousled hair of his *petite chérie*.

So that was what he did.

XVIII

THE FOLLOWING WEEK BROUGHT NO MORE NEWS OF CLÉMENCE. By three every afternoon, Danglard was drifting off into an alcoholic haze, punctuated by a few verbal outbursts to vent his frustration. Dozens of reported sightings of her had come in. Morning after morning, Danglard would place on Adamsberg's desk the negative results of the follow-up searches.

'Report from Montauban. False alarm again,' said Danglard.

And Adamsberg had raised his head to say, 'Fine, OK, very good.' Worse still, Danglard suspected that Adamsberg was not even reading the reports. In the evening, they were still sitting where Danglard had left them in the morning. So he picked them up again and filed them away in the dossier marked 'Clémence Valmont'.

Danglard couldn't help keeping count. It had been twenty-seven days now since Clémence Valmont had disappeared. Mathilde often telephoned Adamsberg to see if there was any news of her weird little shrew-mouse, and Danglard heard him say, 'No, nothing. No, I haven't given up, what makes you think so? I'm waiting for some facts to trickle in. No hurry.'

'No hurry.' Adamsberg's motto. Danglard was in a state of high nervous tension, whereas Castreau seemed to have changed his spots and was taking life as it came, with unusual tolerance for him.

In addition to this, Reyer had come in several times at Adamsberg's request. Danglard found him less off-putting than before. He wondered whether that was because Reyer was more familiar with the police station now that he could find his way along the corridors by feeling the walls, or because the identification of the murderer had left him feeling relieved. What Danglard did not want to think, at any cost, was that the handsome blind man was in a better mood because he had found his way to Mathilde's bed. No, anything but that. How would he know, though? He had listened to the beginning of his interview with the *commissaire*.

'Take you now,' Adamsberg had said, 'you can't see any more, so you have different ways of seeing. What I'd like is for you to talk to me about Clémence Valmont for as long as you like, just give me your impressions of her, how it struck you when you listened to her, all the sensations you felt in her presence, all the details you guessed at when you went near her, or heard her, or felt she was in the room. The more I know about her, the more likely it is I'll get somewhere. You're the person, Reyer, along with Mathilde, who must have known her best. And you have a knowledge of the para-visible. You pick up on all the things that we fail to understand because we get a quick visual fix with our eyes, which satisfies us.'

And every time he came, Reyer stayed there for a long while. Through the open door, Danglard could see Adamsberg leaning against the wall and listening attentively.

*   *   *

It was three-thirty in the afternoon. Adamsberg opened his notebook at page three. He waited for a long-drawn-out moment, then wrote as follows:

Tomorrow I'll go out into the country to look for Clémence. I don't think I'm mistaken. I can't remember when it came to me, I should have made a note. Was it at the very beginning? Or when I heard about the smell of rotten apples? Everything Reyer tells me points in the same direction. Yesterday I took a walk as far as the Gare de l'Est. I wondered why I was a policeman. Perhaps because it's a job where you have to look for things with some chance of finding them, and that makes up for the rest. Because in the rest of your life, nobody ever asks you to look for anything and you don't stand much chance of finding anything, since you don't know what you're looking for. Leaves, for instance. I don't know why it is, really, that I keep drawing them. Yesterday in the café in the Gare de l'Est, someone said to me that the way not to be afraid of death was to live as stupid a life as possible. That way there'd be nothing to regret. It didn't seem a very good solution to me.

But I'm not afraid of death, not all that much. So it didn't really concern me, what he said. And I'm not afraid of being lonely either.

All my shirts need replacing, now I think of it. What I'd like is to find some sort of universal clothing. Then I'd buy thirty sets and I wouldn't have to worry about clothes for the rest of my life. When I told my sister what I thought, she shrieked. The very idea of a universal uniform horrified her.

I'd like to find a universal uniform so that I wouldn't have to think about it.

I'd like to find a universal leaf too, so that I wouldn't have to bother about that.

When it comes down to it, I wish I hadn't missed Camille the other night in the street. I'd have caught up with her, she'd have been astonished – touched, perhaps. I might have seen her face tremble, she might have blushed or turned pale, I don't know which. I would have taken her face in my hands to stop her trembling, and it would have been fantastic. I'd have held her in my arms, we'd have stood there in the street for a long time. An hour, say. But perhaps she wouldn't have felt anything at all. Perhaps she wouldn't have wanted to stand there holding me. Perhaps she wouldn't have wanted to have anything to do with me. I don't know. I can't imagine. Perhaps she'd have said, 'Jean-Baptiste, my taxi's waiting.' I don't know. And perhaps it wasn't Camille at all. And perhaps I don't care. I don't know. I don't think so.

And as for my intellectual colleague Danglard, I'm getting on his nerves. It's obvious. I'm not doing it on purpose. Nothing's happening, nothing's being said, and that's what gets on his nerves. And yet since Clémence has gone missing, some key thing has happened. But I couldn't tell him.

Adamsberg raised his head as he heard the door open.

It was a warm afternoon. Danglard was returning from a northern suburb, perspiring freely. An interview about stolen goods. It had been quite satisfactory, but it hadn't satisfied him. Danglard needed more important cases to keep him going, and the murderous shrew-mouse seemed to him to be a worthy challenge. But the fear of having to admit failure was getting sharper every day. He didn't even dare talk about the case to the children. He was feeling very much like pouring himself a glass of white wine, when Adamsberg came into his office.

'I'm looking for some scissors,' Adamsberg said.

Danglard went to look in Florence's desk and found a pair. He noticed that Florence had laid in a fresh stock of toffees. Adamsberg closed one eye as he threaded a needle.

'What's up now?' asked Danglard. 'Bit of mending?'

'The hem of my trousers has come undone.'

Adamsberg sat on a chair, crossed his knee and began to mend his trousers. Danglard watched him, taken somewhat aback, but feeling soothed. It was soothing to watch someone sewing with little stitches, as if the rest of the world didn't exist.

'You'll see how good I am at this, Danglard,' Adamsberg remarked. 'I do tiny little stitches. My youngest sister showed me how, one day when we didn't know what to do with ourselves, as my father used to say.'

'*I* don't know what to do with myself,' said Danglard. 'For one thing, I'm no good at fixing the hems on the kids' trousers. And for another, this killer is haunting me. Ghastly, horrible old woman. She's going to get away, I know it. It's driving me nuts. Honestly, it's driving me nuts.'

He got up to take a beer can out of the cupboard.

'No,' said Adamsberg

'No what?'

'No beer.'

The *commissaire* was biting off the thread, having completely forgotten that he had Florence's scissors.

'The scissors are right there,' said Danglard. 'Damn it all, I fetched you the scissors for the thread, and look what you're doing now. And what's wrong with beer, all of a sudden?'

'What's wrong is that you might get launched and drink ten beers, and today that won't do.'

'I didn't think that was any of your business. My body, my responsibility, my belly and my beer.'

'Of course. But it's your investigation and you're my inspector. And tomorrow we're going to the country. We have a rendezvous with someone we know, I hope. So I need you, and I need you with a clear head. And a strong stomach, too. Very important, the stomach. I don't know if a settled stomach helps one to think clearly. But I do know that a poor stomach will stop you thinking at all.'

Danglard observed Adamsberg's tense face. It was impossible to guess whether it was because his thread had just knotted, or because of the projected trip to the country.

'Oh damn and blast!' said Adamsberg. 'My thread's got a knot. I really hate that. Apparently the golden rule is that you should sew in the same direction as it comes off the reel, otherwise you get a knot. See what I mean? I must have been working the other way without thinking. And now there's a knot.'

'I think you had too long a thread in the first place,' Danglard ventured.

Yes, sewing was a restful kind of occupation.

'No, Danglard, I had the right length, from my hand to my elbow. Tomorrow, at eight o'clock, I'll need eight men, a van and some dogs. And we'd better take the doctor along too.'

He poked the needle into the knot to undo it, broke off

the thread, and smoothed down his trousers. Then he went out, without discovering whether Danglard would have a clear head and a strong stomach the next day. Danglard didn't know, either.

XIX

CHARLES REYER WAS ON HIS WAY HOME. HE WAS FEELING RELAXED and enjoying it while it lasted. His conversations with Adamsberg had brought him some tranquillity, though he didn't know why. All he knew was that for the last two days he had not tried to help anyone else to cross the road.

He had even managed, without having to make much of an effort, to speak sincerely to the *commissaire* about Clémence, about Mathilde, and about a multitude of other things, taking his time. Adamsberg had told him things too. Things about himself. Not always very clear. Some were trivial, some were serious, but he wasn't sure that the trivial ones weren't in fact the more serious ones. It was hard to tell with Adamsberg. The wisdom of a child, the philosophy of an old man. As he had said to Mathilde in the restaurant. He had not been wrong about what was conveyed by the *commissaire's* gentle voice. And then the *commissaire* had asked him what was going on behind his dark eyes. He had told him, and Adamsberg had listened. All the sounds a blind man hears, all his painful perceptions in the dark, all the visibility that the blackness brings him. When he stopped, Adamsberg would say: 'Go on,

Reyer, I'm listening.' Charles imagined that if he had been a woman he could have fallen in love with Adamsberg, while feeling despair that he was so elusive. But he was the kind of man it was probably best not to get too close to. Or else you had to be prepared not to be in despair at his elusiveness. Or something like that.

But Charles was a man, and he liked being a man. What was more, Adamsberg had confirmed the view that he was good-looking. Being a man, therefore, Charles thought he would have liked to be in love with Mathilde.

~~Since he was after all a man.~~

But was Mathilde trying to lose herself, under the sea? Was she trying not to have to hear anything of earthly battles? What had happened to Mathilde? Nobody knew. Why was she so keen on the bloody water? Could anyone catch hold of Mathilde? Charles was afraid she would slip away like a mermaid.

He didn't stop at his landing, but went straight up to the Flying Gurnard. He felt for the bell push and rang twice.

'Something wrong?' asked Mathilde, opening the door. 'Or is there any news about the shrew-mouse?'

'Would I know if there was?'

'You've been to see Adamsberg a few times, haven't you? I called him just now. Seems there'll be some news about Clémence tomorrow.'

'Why are you so interested in Clémence?'

'Because I found her. She's *my* shrew-mouse.'

'No, *she* found *you*. Why've you been crying, Mathilde?'

'Crying? Yes, I have a bit. How do you know?'

'Your voice sounds a bit damp still. I can hear it perfectly.'

'Don't worry. It's just that someone I love very much is leaving tomorrow. That makes me cry just now.'

'Can I find out what your face looks like?' asked Charles, stretching out his hands.

'How?'

'Like this. You'll see.'

Charles stretched his fingers out to Mathilde's face, and ran them across it like a pianist on a keyboard. He was concentrating hard. In fact, he knew perfectly well what Mathilde looked like. She probably hadn't changed much from the seminars when he had seen her. But he wanted to touch her. It was the first time they had called each other 'tu'.

would never find out. Yes, it had been entertaining. A first section.

But this morning she had no interest in anything. Towards the end of a first section, one shouldn't expect too much. She thought that this was the day when Jean-Baptiste Adamsberg was going to catch the shrew-mouse, that she would struggle and make a squeaking noise, and that it was going to be the devil of a day for old Clémence, who had been so good at sorting out the slides with her gloves on, just as she had sorted out her murders. Mathilde wondered for a moment if she ought to feel responsible. If she hadn't been showing off at the *Dodin Bouffant*, boasting that she knew about the chalk circle man, Clémence wouldn't have come to lodge with her, and wouldn't have been able to seize the opportunity to murder people. Then she told herself, no, wait a minute, the whole idea was just too far-fetched. For a woman to cut the throat of an elderly doctor just because he had once been her fiancé, and for pent-up bitterness to have done the rest.

Too far-fetched by half. She should have told Adamsberg that. Mathilde was muttering her sentences to herself as she leaned on her aquarium-table. 'Adamsberg, this murder is just too far-fetched.' A crime of passion doesn't take place in cold blood fifty years later, especially with a plan as complicated as that worked out by Clémence. How could Adamsberg be so wrong about the old woman's motive? You'd have to be stupid to believe in a motive as far-fetched as that. And what bothered Mathilde was precisely that she considered Adamsberg to be one of the subtlest people she had ever met. Yet there was obviously something wrong about the motive they were assigning to Clémence. A woman with a blank face. Mathilde had tried to convince herself that Clémence was likeable, in order to try and like her and help her, but in fact everything about the shrew-mouse had set her teeth on edge. Everything – or rather nothing: it was as if there was no body inside her body, no expression on her face, no sound in her voice. Just nothingness.

Last night, Charles had felt her face with his fingers. It had been rather nice, she had to admit, those long hands scrupulously exploring all the contours of her face, as if she were printed out in Braille. She had sensed that he might have liked to go further, but she had not given him any encouragement. On the contrary, she had made some coffee. Very good coffee, in fact. That was no substitute for a caress, of course. But in a way a caress is no substitute for a good cup of coffee, either. Mathilde shook herself: the comparison was silly, caresses and good cups of coffee were not interchangeable.

'Right,' she sighed out loud. With her finger she was following a two-spot Lepadogaster swimming under the glass lid. Time to feed the fish. What was she to do with Charles and his caresses? Was it time perhaps for her to go back to the sea, since she didn't feel like following anybody this morning? What had she collected in three months? A policeman who should have been a prostitute, a malicious blind man who caressed her, a Byzantine scholar who drew chalk circles, and an old murderess. Not a bad haul, after all. She shouldn't complain. Rather, she should write it all down. That would be more fun than writing about pectoral fins.

'Yes, but what?' she said out loud, standing up abruptly. 'What could I write? What's the point of writing?'

'To tell the story of your life,' she answered herself.

Stuff and nonsense! At least when you're dealing with

pectoral fins you've got something to say that other people don't know. But as for anything else, why bother? Why do anything or write anything? To attract others? Is that it? To seduce people you've never met, as if the ones you have met aren't enough for you? Because you think you can capture the quintessence of the world in a few pages? What quintessence is there, anyway? What emotions are there in the world? What can you say? Even the story of the old shrew-mouse isn't interesting enough to tell anyone. Writing is an admission of failure.

Mathilde sat down again in a dark mood. She decided that her thinking had become muddled. Pectoral fins are absolutely fine, nothing wrong with them.

But it's depressing if all you write about is pectoral fins, because in the end you couldn't give a damn about them, any more than you do about Clémence.

Mathilde sat up and pushed her dark hair back with both hands. Right, she thought, I'm just having a little attack of metaphysics and it will pass. 'Stuff and nonsense,' she muttered again. I wouldn't be so sad if Camille wasn't leaving again tonight. Off again. If only she hadn't met that slippery policeman, she wouldn't be obliged to travel the world. And is it worth writing that down?

No.

Perhaps it really was time to go back to the depths of the ocean. And above all, it was forbidden to ask herself what the point of it all was.

'What is the point of it all?' Mathilde immediately asked herself.

To do you good. To get your feet wet. Yes, that was it. To get your feet wet.

*　*　*

Adamsberg was driving fast. Danglard had gathered they were going to Montargis, but he knew no more than that. The further they travelled, the tenser the *commissaire*'s features became. And the contrasts marking his face became almost unreal. Adamsberg's face was like one of those lamps that have dimmer switches. Very odd. What Danglard did not understand at all was why Adamsberg had put a black tie on over his old white shirt. A tie for a funeral, but knotted any old how. Danglard voiced his concern.

'Yes,' said Adamsberg. 'I did put this tie on. It's a fitting custom, isn't it?'

And that was all. Except for the hand which he sometimes laid on Danglard's arm. More than two hours out of Paris, Adamsberg stopped the car on a forest track. Here the summer heat failed to penetrate. Danglard read a notice: *Bertranges Forestry Estate*, and Adamsberg said, 'This is it,' as he put on the handbrake.

He got out of the car, took a deep breath and looked around, with a nod. Spreading a map on the bonnet, he called Castreau, Delille and the six men from the van to come over.

'We'll go this way,' he said, pointing. 'We take this track, then this one and the next. Then we'll check all the paths in the southern sector. What we're going to do is search the zone around this lodge in the forest.'

At the same time, his finger described a circle on the map.

'Circles, always circles,' he murmured.

He crumpled the map up clumsily and gave it to Castreau.

'Get the dogs out,' he added.

Six Alsatians on leads jumped out of the van, barking furiously. Danglard, who didn't greatly care for the huge beasts, kept to one side, folding his arms and keeping the folds of his floppy grey jacket pulled tight round him as his only protection.

'All this palaver to track down old Clémence?' he said. 'But how will the dogs manage it, anyway? We don't even have a scrap of her clothing for them to sniff.'

'I've got what we need,' said Adamsberg, taking a small packet from the van and putting it down in front of the dogs.

'Ugh, rotten meat,' said Delille, wrinkling his nose.

'Smells of death,' said Castreau.

'Yes,' said Adamsberg.

He jerked his head and they took the first track on the right. The dogs were pulling hard on their leads and barking. One of them had already wolfed down the piece of meat.

'Dumb creature, that dog,' said Castreau.

'I don't like this at all,' said Danglard.

'No, I thought not,' said Adamsberg.

Walking through a forest with dogs is a noisy process. Branches and twigs cracking, little creatures running from underfoot, startled bird-calls, and the constant sound of feet crunching on leaves and dogs crashing through undergrowth.

Adamsberg was wearing his faithful black trousers. He walked along with his hands partly tucked into his belt, the tie flying back over one shoulder, saying nothing, but attending to the slightest deviation by the dogs. Three-quarters of an hour passed before two of the dogs simultaneously left the path, taking a sharp left turn. There was no track there, just undergrowth. They had to push under branches and round tree trunks, making slow progress, with the dogs pulling at the lead. A branch snapped back painfully into Danglard's face. The leading dog, Alarm Clock by name but usually known just as 'Clock', stopped after they had gone about sixty metres. He turned round in his tracks, barking and raising his head, then whined and lay on the ground, his head held upright, looking pleased with himself. Adamsberg had frozen, his fingers locked on his belt. He looked at the small patch of ground where Clock was lying, a few square metres between the birches and the oaks. He reached out and touched a branch that had been broken several months earlier. Moss had grown on the broken end.

His mouth twisted, as it always did when he felt a powerful emotion. Danglard had noticed that before.

'Call the others,' Adamsberg said.

Then he watched, as Declerc brought up the bag of tools and signalled that they could start work. Danglard watched apprehensively as Declerc opened the bag and brought out pickaxes and shovels, which he distributed to the others.

For an hour he had been refusing to think that this was what they were looking for. But now he could no longer escape the evidence. This *was* what they were looking for.

'A rendezvous with someone we know,' Adamsberg had said the day before. The black tie. So the *commissaire* did not shrink from symbolism, however heavy-handed.

After that, the shovels started to make an infernal noise as metal struck on stone, a sound that Danglard had heard too many times in the past. The pile of earth alongside grew higher. He'd seen that too many times as well. The men were practised at digging. They worked quickly, bending their knees.

Adamsberg, still gazing fixedly at the growing hole, touched Declerc on the arm.

'Take it slower now. Not too hard. Use the smaller shovels.'

They had to move the dogs away – they were making too much noise.

'The mutts are getting excited,' Castreau observed. Adamsberg nodded, continuing to stare into the hole. Declerc was directing operations. He was lifting earth gingerly with a light trowel. Suddenly he sprang back as if he had been attacked. He wiped his nose with his sleeve.

'Ah, look,' he said. 'A hand, I think. I think it's a hand.'

Danglard made a prodigious effort to detach himself from the tree trunk against which he was leaning, and approached the pit. Yes, it was a hand. A ghastly, terrible hand.

Now one man was uncovering the arm, another the head, and a third shreds of blue fabric. Danglard felt sick. He moved back, reaching behind him with his hand to find the tree trunk, his solid oak tree. He felt its bark and clung to it, as his eyes continued to see the image he had glimpsed of a horrible corpse, with black slimy skin.

I should never have come, he thought, closing his eyes. And he did not even want to know for the moment whose corpse the ghastly thing could be, or why they had come to look for it, or where they were, and why he didn't understand. All he knew was that the *commissaire* must be wrong about the rendezvous. That corpse had been there for months. So whoever it was, it couldn't be Clémence.

The men worked on for another hour, with the stench becoming intolerable. Danglard had not shifted an inch from his comforting oak tree. He kept his gaze fixed upwards. Between the trees you could only see a little bit of sky and this corner of the forest was dark. He heard Adamsberg say gently:

'That'll do for now. Let's have a drink.'

The men threw down the tools and Declerc produced a bottle of cognac from the bag.

'It's nothing fancy,' he explained, 'but it'll disinfect us a bit. Just a drop each.'

'Against the rules, but indispensable,' said Adamsberg.

The *commissaire* walked over to Danglard, holding a plastic cup. He didn't say 'How are you doing?' or 'Feeling better now?' In fact, he said nothing. He knew it would be all right in half an hour, and Danglard would be able to walk again. Everyone knew about his squeamishness, and no one blamed him for it. They were quite busy enough with their own internal struggles around the foul-smelling pit.

The nine men sat a little way from the excavation, near Danglard who remained standing. The doctor, who had been prowling round the pit, came to join them.

'So, Dr Death,' said Castreau, 'what does all this tell you?'

'It tells me that it was a woman, elderly, sixty or seventy perhaps. And she was killed by a wound to the throat, getting on for six months ago, I'd say. It's going to be hard work identifying her, lads.' (The pathologist often said 'lads', as if he were teaching a class.) 'The clothes look like ordinary mass-produced stuff, they won't help us. I don't think we've got any personal items in the grave, either. And there's not much hope the dental records will give us anything. She had perfect teeth, like you and me, no fillings, no dental work at all, as far as I can see. That's what it tells me, lads. So you're going to be hard put to it to find out who she is.'

'She's Clémence Valmont,' Adamsberg said quietly. 'Domiciled in Neuilly-sur-Seine. Aged sixty-four. Let me have another drop of cognac, Declerc. It's not marvellous, you're right, but it hits the spot.'

'No!' said Danglard, more vehemently than they would have expected, though without budging from his tree. 'No!

It can't be! The doctor's just told us that this woman's been dead for months. And Clémence only left the rue des Patriarches in Paris a month ago, alive and well. So how can it be her?'

'You didn't listen,' Adamsberg said. 'I said Clémence Valmont, domiciled in Neuilly-sur-Seine. Not domiciled in the rue des Patriarches.'

'So what do you mean?' asked Castreau. 'Are there two of them? Two people with the same name? Or twins?'

Adamsberg shook his head, swirling the cognac round the bottom of the cup.

'There was only ever one,' he said. 'Clémence Valmont who lived in Neuilly and who was murdered five or six months ago. That's her,' he said, jerking his chin at the grave. 'And then there was someone *else* who had been living for two months at Mathilde Forestier's house in the rue des Patriarches, under the name of Clémence Valmont. Someone who had killed Clémence Valmont.'

'But who?' asked Delille.

Adamsberg glanced at Danglard before replying, as if to apologise.

'A man,' he said. 'The chalk circle man.'

They had moved away from the open grave, so as to breathe more freely. Two men took it in turns to do the work. They were now waiting for the technical team to arrive, and the local *commissaire* from Nevers. Adamsberg had sat down with Castreau beside the van, and Danglard had gone for a walk.

He walked around for half an hour, letting the sun warm his back and restore his lost strength. So the shrew-mouse had been the chalk circle man. The same man who had cut the throats in turn of Clémence Valmont, Madeleine Châtelain, Gérard Pontieux and finally his own wife. Inside his rat-like brain, he had worked out his infernal plan. First of all the circles. Plenty of circles. Everyone thought they were the work of a lunatic. A pathetic maniac who was exploited by a killer. Everything had happened the way he had planned. He had been arrested, and ended up confessing to his mania for doing circles. Just as he had planned. Then he had been released, and everyone had gone chasing after Clémence. The guilty party he had been grooming. Clémence, who had been dead for months, and whom they would have gone on searching for indefinitely, until they had to abandon the case as unsolved. Danglard frowned. Too many things seemed inexplicable.

He rejoined the *commissaire* who was silently munching some bread with Castreau, both of them seated at the edge of the track. Castreau was trying to attract a hen blackbird with a few breadcrumbs.

'Why is it,' Castreau was saying, 'that the females are always duller-looking than the males? Hen birds are all brown or beige, or some other boring colour. As if they couldn't care less. But the males are red and green and gold. Why on earth should that be? It looks the wrong way round.'

'What they say is,' said Adamsberg, 'that the males need to make all that fuss to attract a mate. They have to keep on inventing stuff. I don't know if you've noticed that, Castreau. All the time, inventing new stuff. Exhausting.'

The hen blackbird flew off.

'Well, the female's got enough to do, inventing eggs and bringing them up, hasn't she?' said Delille.

'Like me,' said Danglard. 'I must be a hen blackbird. My

eggs give me plenty of headaches, especially the youngest one, who was dumped on me, like a cuckoo in the nest.'

'Ah, but hold on,' said Castreau. 'You don't wear brown and beige.'

'Anyway, for God's sake,' said Danglard, 'ornithology is beside the point. You won't understand people by observing birds. Birds are bloody birds, that's all there is to it. So why are we talking about them when we've got a *corpse* here and we don't understand the first thing about what's going on? At least I don't. But perhaps you all know everything about everything?'

Danglard was aware that he was going too far, and in other circumstances would have defended a more moderate point of view. But he wasn't feeling strong enough for that this morning.

'You'll have to forgive me for not keeping you filled in on everything,' Adamsberg said to Danglard. 'But until this morning I really wasn't sure of myself. I didn't want to take you off on a wild-goose chase just because I had a sort of hunch, which you would have torn to pieces by applying reason to it. Your cast-iron reasoning influences me, Danglard, and I didn't want to take the risk of being influenced until this morning. Or I might have lost the scent.'

'The scent of rotten apples?'

'Well, in particular the scent of the circles. Those circles that I really hated. I hated them even more when Vercors-Laury confirmed that we weren't dealing with some authentic compulsion. Worse, there was no sign of obsession at all. Nothing about the circles indicated a genuine obsession. The whole thing just *looked* like an obsession, like the conventional idea someone might have about it. For instance, Danglard, it was you who pointed out that the man varied his technique: sometimes he drew the circle in a single line, but other times in two pieces, or even an oval. Would a real maniac have tolerated such sloppiness, do you think? A real obsessive sets out his little world very precisely, to the millimetre. Otherwise there's no point having an obsession at all. An obsession is a way of organising the world, to bring it under control, to possess the impossible, so as to protect yourself from it. So a lot of circles like that, on any old date, with any old object in them, without any pattern to the place or the technique, could only be a fake obsession. And the oval circle in the rue Bertholet, around Delphine Le Nermord, was a big mistake.'

'How do you mean?' asked Castreau. 'Oh look, here's the male now, yellow beak!'

'The circle was oval, because the pavement was so narrow. Any self-respecting maniac wouldn't have been able to cope with that. He'd have gone three streets up, simply to draw his circle. So if the circle was there, in this street, it was because it had to be, halfway between the two beats of the policemen, and in a dark street where the murder could take place. And the circle was oval, because there was no way of killing Delphine Le Nermord anywhere else – on the boulevard, for instance. Too many cops wandering about, as I said, Danglard. He had to take cover, and kill in a safe place. So too bad about the circle, it would have to be an oval. That's a dramatic mistake for a so-called maniac.'

'Did you realise that night that the circle man was the killer?'

'Well, I did know at least that the circles had something wrong with them. Fake circles.'

'Well, he certainly put on a class act, Le Nermord, didn't

he? He had me round his little finger, with his tears, his panic, his collapse, and then his confession, finally getting me to think he was innocent. All complete bullshit.'

'Yes, he did it very well. He shook you, Danglard. Even the examining magistrate, who isn't a soft touch at all, thought it was impossible that he could be guilty. Killing his wife in one of his own circles just made no sense. So we had no choice but to let him go, and after that we went wherever he wanted us to. He led us by the nose to the murderer he had invented, poor old Clémence. And I was no different. I just went along with it.'

'Now the male's brought a present for the hen,' said Castreau. 'A little strip of tinfoil.'

'Aren't you interested in what we're talking about?' asked Danglard.

'Yes, but I don't want to seem too interested because it makes me feel like an idiot. You didn't take any notice of me, but I was thinking about this case too. The only thing I thought was that Le Nermord was a bit creepy. But I didn't get any further than that. I looked for Clémence like the rest of us.'

'Clémence!' said Adamsberg. 'He must have taken some time to find her. He had to find someone of roughly his own age and build, someone inconspicuous, and sufficiently isolated from other people that her disappearance would go unnoticed. This elderly Mademoiselle Valmont in Neuilly was just the job, a lonely old lady, obsessively answering small ads from the paper. He just had to answer one, charm her, promise her the moon, convince her to sell up and go off with him, with her two suitcases – it wasn't too difficult. Clémence told no one but her neighbours. But since they weren't close friends they weren't too bothered about her adventure, they just had a good laugh about it. Nobody had ever seen the famous new fiancé. And the poor old soul turned up at the rendezvous.'

'Ah,' said Castreau. 'Here comes another male now. What's he want? The female's looking at him, there's going to be a fight. Oh-oh, here we go.'

'So he killed her,' said Danglard. 'Then he brought her all this way to bury her. Why here? Where is this?'

Adamsberg stretched a weary arm out to his left.

'If you're going to bury someone, you have to know a quiet spot. The lodge in the forest is the Le Nermords' country house.'

Danglard looked through the trees at the distant house. Yes, Le Nermord had certainly made a fool of him.

'After that,' Danglard went on, 'he disguised himself as Clémence. Easy enough, he had her two suitcases.'

'Carry on, Danglard, I leave it to you now.'

'Now the hen blackbird's flying away,' said Castreau. 'She's dropped the tinfoil. Waste of time bringing her presents. No, she's coming back.'

'He went to lodge with Mathilde,' said Danglard. 'This woman had been following him. She worried him. He had to keep an eye on Mathilde, and then use her. The empty flat was a stroke of luck. If there was a problem, Mathilde would be a perfect witness: she knew the circle man and she knew Clémence. She believed they were two different people and he worked hard to convince her of that. How did he manage the teeth, though?'

'Well, it was you who remarked on the noise he made with his pipe against his teeth.'

'Yes. Ah, dentures, of course. He must have filed down an

old set. What about the eyes, though? He's got blue eyes. Clémence's were brown. Oh, contact lenses! Yes, tinted contact lenses. Beret, gloves, she was always wearing gloves. But the transformation must have taken a bit of time and a lot of trouble, in fact quite a bit of artistry. And how could he leave his own house dressed as an old woman? One of his neighbours might have seen him. Where did he change?'

'He changed somewhere on the way. He left his house as a man and arrived in the rue des Patriarches as a woman. And vice versa, of course.'

'So where did he do it? Some abandoned house, a workman's hut perhaps, where he could change and leave the clothes?'

'Something like that. We'll have to find it. He'll have to tell us.'

'A workman's hut, that makes sense, with bits of rotten food left behind, old wine bottles, a mildewy sort of enclosed space. Was that it, the smell? The smell of rotten apples that hung about his clothes? But why didn't Clémence's clothes smell the same, then?'

'Her clothes were very light. He could keep them on under his suit, and he put the beret and gloves in his briefcase. But he couldn't keep his man's clothes under Clémence's, of course. So he had to leave them behind.'

'My God, what a carry-on! Think of the organisation.'

'For some people, organisation is delicious in itself. This was a sophisticated murder, one that meant months of preparatory work. He started doing his circles more than four months before we found the first victim. This kind of Byzantine scholar wouldn't be put off by hours and hours of meticulous preparation, working it out. I'm sure he enjoyed it all immensely. For instance, the idea of using Gérard Pontieux to make us start running after Clémence. The kind of imbroglio he must have relished. And the drop of blood deposited in Clémence's flat, the finishing touch before she disappeared.'

'But, Christ Almighty, where is he now?'

'He's gone into town. He'll be back at lunchtime. There's no hurry, he's completely sure of himself. A plan as complicated as this couldn't go wrong. But he didn't know about the fashion magazine. His Delphie was taking some liberties that she didn't tell him about.'

'The smaller male has won,' said Castreau. 'I'm going to give him some bread. He's worked hard for it.'

Adamsberg looked up. The lab team was arriving. Conti got down from the truck with all his paraphernalia.

'You'll see,' said Danglard, greeting Conti. 'No hairpins this time. But the same guy did it.'

'And we're going after him now', said Adamsberg, standing up.

XXI

AUGUSTIN-LOUIS LE NERMORD'S HOUSE WAS AN OLD AND RATHER ramshackle hunting lodge. Over the front door was nailed the skull of a stag.

'Jolly place!' said Danglard.

'Ah, jolly's not the word that comes to mind, is it?' said Adamsberg. 'He's got a taste for death. Reyer told me that about Clémence. The most important thing he told me was that she talked like a man.'

'See if I care,' said Castreau. 'Look at this.'

He proudly displayed the hen blackbird, who was now sitting on his shoulder.

'Ever seen that before? A tame blackbird, and she's chosen me.'

Castreau laughed.

'I'm going to call her Breadcrumb,' he said. 'Daft, isn't it? Do you think she'll stay?'

Adamsberg rang the doorbell. They heard the sound of slippers approaching unhurriedly in the corridor. Le Nermord clearly suspected nothing. When he opened the door,

Danglard had a different take on his washed-out blue eyes, and his pale skin marked with liver spots.

'I was just about to eat,' said Le Nermord. 'What's happened?'

'It's all over, monsieur,' said Adamsberg. 'These things happen.'

He put a hand on the professor's shoulder.

'You're hurting me,' said Le Nermord, recoiling.

'Come with us, please,' said Castreau. 'You're charged with four murders.'

The blackbird was still sitting on his shoulder as he took Le Nermord's wrists and slipped the handcuffs over them. In the past, under his former boss, Castreau used to boast that he could cuff a suspect before they had time to notice. In this case, he said nothing.

Danglard had not taken his stare off the circle man. And he seemed now to understand what Adamsberg had meant with his story of the drooling dog. The identification of cruelty. It seemed to seep from every pore. The chalk circle man had become terrible to see in the space of a minute. Even more ghastly than the corpse in the grave.

XXII

By evening, everyone was back in Paris. There was an atmosphere of overwork and excitement in the station. The chalk circle man, being held down on a chair by Declerc and Margellon, was spitting out a stream of foul language.

'Hear him?' Danglard asked Adamsberg as he went into the *commissaire*'s office.

For once, Adamsberg wasn't doodling. He was finishing off his report to the examining magistrate, standing up.

'Yes, I hear him,' said Adamsberg.

'He wants to cut *your* throat.'

'Yes, I know, *mon vieux*. You ought to call Mathilde Forestier. She'll want to know what happened to the shrew-mouse – it's understandable.'

Delighted with his task, Danglard went out to phone.

'She's not there,' he reported on his return. 'I just got Reyer. He gets on my nerves, Reyer does, he's in her flat all the time. Mathilde has gone to see someone off on the nine o'clock train from the Gare du Nord. He thinks she'll be back right away. He said she wasn't feeling too good, there was a break in her voice, and perhaps we should go round later to have a drink and cheer her up. But how would we cheer her up?'

Adamsberg was staring hard at Danglard.

'What's the time?' he asked.

'Twenty past eight. Why?'

Adamsberg snatched up his jacket and ran out of the room. Danglard had time to hear him call over his shoulder, telling him to check the report while he was away and that he'd be back.

Adamsberg ran down the street, trying to find a taxi. He managed to reach the Gare du Nord by a quarter to nine. Still running, he went in through the main entrance, reaching for a cigarette at the same time. He bumped into Mathilde coming out.

'Quick, Mathilde, quick! She's going away, isn't she? Don't lie to me, for God's sake! I know she's here! What platform? Tell me what platform!'

Mathilde looked at him in silence.

'What platform?' shouted Adamsberg.

'Hell and damnation, Adamsberg!' said Mathilde. 'Go away, get lost. If it wasn't for you, perhaps she wouldn't keep running off all the time.'

'You don't know her! She's just like that! The platform, for God's sake!'

Mathilde didn't want to tell him.

'Fourteen,' she said.

Adamsberg abandoned her. It was six minutes to nine by the station clock. He drew breath as he approached Platform Fourteen.

Yes, she was there. Of course. In a tight black sweater and skirt. Like a shadow. Camille was standing up very straight, her gaze lost somewhere – watching the whole station, perhaps. Adamsberg remembered that expression: wanting to see everything, expecting nothing. She was holding a cigarette.

Then she threw it away. Camille always had very elegant gestures. An effective one in this case. She picked up her suitcase and walked along the platform. Adamsberg ran along in front of her, and turned to face her. Camille bumped into him.

'Come with me,' he said. 'You've got to come. Just for an hour.'

Camille looked at him. She was touched, exactly as he had imagined she would have been if he had caught up with her at the taxi.

'No,' she said. 'Go away, Jean-Baptiste.'

Camille looked unsteady. Adamsberg remembered that even in normal circumstances she always gave the impression that she was about to somersault or fly into the air. Rather like her mother. As if she was balancing along a plank above a space rather than walking on the ground like everyone else. But now Camille was actually swaying to and fro.

'Camille, you're not going to fall over, are you? Are you?'

'No, no.'

Camille put down the suitcase and stretched her arms over her head as if to reach for the sky.

'Look at me, Jean-Baptiste. I'm on tiptoe, see. I'm not going to fall.'

Camille smiled and let fall her arms, breathing out.

'I love you. But let me go now.'

She threw her case in at the open carriage door. She climbed the three steps and turned round, a slim black shape, and

Adamsberg did not want there to be only seconds left for him to look at this face in which a Greek god and an Egyptian prostitute were somehow combined.

Camille shook her head.

'You know how it is, Jean-Baptiste. I was in love with you, and it doesn't go away if you just blow. Flies go away if you just blow on them. But I'll tell you something: you're nothing like a fly. God, no. But I don't have the strength to go on loving someone like you. It's too difficult. It breaks me up. I never know where you are, where your soul has gone off to. And my own soul flits about as well. So everyone's upset, all the time. You know all this, for God's sake, Jean-Baptiste.'

Camille smiled.

The doors closed, loudspeakers told people to stand back. Passengers were admonished not to throw things out of the windows. Yes, Adamsberg knew all that. Your thoughtless action may maim or kill. The train was about to leave.

One hour. Just one hour, before leaving this world.

He ran after the train, gripped the rail and hauled himself up.

'Police!' he said to the guard who was about to shout at him.

He walked halfway along the train.

He found her lying on a single couchette, leaning on her elbow, neither sleeping nor reading, nor crying. He went in and shut the door of the compartment.

'As I have always thought,' said Camille. 'You're a trouble-maker.'

'I just want to lie down beside you for an hour.'

'Why for an hour?'

'I don't know.'

'You still say "I don't know" to every question?'

'I still do everything. I still love you. I still want to lie down with you.'

'No, it'll upset me too much afterwards.'

'You're right. Same here.'

They sat facing each other for a while. The ticket collector came in.

'Police,' said Adamsberg. 'I'm questioning this lady. Don't let anyone come in. What's the first stop?'

'Lille, two hours.'

'Thank you,' said Adamsberg. He smiled at the ticket collector, so as not to offend him.

Camille had stood up and was looking at the landscape as it flashed past the window.

'It's known as an abuse of power,' said Adamsberg. 'I'm sorry.'

'An hour, you said?'

Camille leaned her forehead against the window.

'Do you think we have any choice?'

'None at all. Sincerely,' said Adamsberg.

Camille leaned against him. Adamsberg held her tight, like in the dream where the bellhop came in. What was good about the train was that the bellhop wasn't there. Nor was Mathilde, who might have pulled her away.

'Lille's in *two* hours,' said Camille.

'An hour for you, and an hour for me,' said Adamsberg.

A few minutes before Lille, Adamsberg dressed in the dark. Then he helped Camille to get dressed, slowly. True enough, neither of them was feeling happy.

'Goodbye, my love,' he said.

He stroked her hair and kissed her.

He didn't want to watch the train as it pulled out. He stayed on the platform, his arms folded. He realised that he had left his jacket in the compartment. He imagined that Camille had perhaps put it on, and that its sleeves fell down over her fingers, that she would look pretty like that, that she had opened the window and was watching the countryside go by in the night. But he wasn't in the train, so he didn't know what Camille was doing now. He wanted to walk out and find a hotel near the station. He would see his *petite chérie* again. For an hour. Let's say one more hour before the end of his life.

The hotel manager said the only available room looked out on the railway. He said that didn't matter.

'Danglard, this is Adamsberg. Have you still got Le Nermord sitting there? He's not asleep? Good. Tell him I won't give him the satisfaction of dying for now. No, that wasn't the reason I called. It's because of the fashion magazine. Read the magazine, read all the articles by Delphine Vitruel. Then read the books by the great historian of Byzantium again. You'll see then that she wrote his books for him. All on her own. All he did was put the documentation together. And with her vegetarian lover backing her up, Delphine was sooner or later going to kick against the pricks. As Le Nermord well knew. She would end up daring to speak out. And then everyone would know that the famous historian had never existed, and that she had been the one who did the thinking and writing for him. His wife. Everyone would know that he was useless, a pathetic domestic tyrant, a rat. That was the motive, Danglard, nothing else. Tell him killing Delphie didn't solve anything. And I hope it kills him.'

'You sound very hard-hearted tonight,' said Danglard. 'Where are you?'

'I'm in Lille. And I'm not feeling happy, not happy at all, *mon vieux*. But it'll pass. It'll go over, I'm sure. You'll see. Back tomorrow, Danglard.'

Camille was smoking in the corridor, her hands deep in the sleeves of Jean-Baptiste's jacket. She didn't want to look at the landscape. In a few moments she would be out of France. She would try to stay calm. After the frontier.

Lying on his hotel bed, Adamsberg was waiting to fall asleep, his hands clasped behind his head. He switched the lamp back on, and pulled his notebook from his back pocket. He didn't think it really helped. But still.

With a pencil he wrote:

'Am in bed in hotel room in Lille. Have lost my jacket.'

He stopped and thought. Yes, it was true he was in bed in Lille.

Then he added:

'Can't sleep. So I'm taking my time, lying on this bed, thinking about my life.'